Twenty-Four Caprices for Violin

and

Caprice d' Adieu

Twenty-Four Caprices for Violin

and

Caprice d' Adieu

by

Emanuel E. Garcia

caprice, n. A work of irregular and sportive fancy
Oxford English Dictionary

"Sometimes a violin is more than a violin."
Anonymous

TABLE OF CONTENTS

Violin Caprice No. 1

'Mendelssohn, Mendelssohn, Mendelssohn, Mendelssohn, Mendelssohn, Mendelssohn. Can this really be?'

Donato touched the speed-dial on his newly acquired mobile device.

'Donato, caro!' answered the peculiar voice on the other end. Werner, Donato's agent, possessed an accent that drifted between Montenegro, Kiev and Istanbul, despite his having hailed from Oxford Circle in Northeast Philadelphia.

'Werner!' exclaimed the violinist petulantly, 'I have fifty-five performances of the Mendelssohn over the next two years – Mendelssohn, Mendelssohn, Mendelssohn!' He shouted into the phone, not knowing exactly where to direct his voice for maximum effect. 'Sibelius once, Brahms twice, Tchaikovsky at a benefit concert and Beethoven not at all!'

'Yes, yes,' replied Werner suavely, 'the demand is so *huge*, Donato, the public cannot get enough of your greatness in the Mendelssohn.'

'And what about my greatness in the Beethoven, in the Dvořák, what about the *Caprices*, and what about my Bach, my Bach? Where are the concerts I have begged you to arrange for solo violin?'

Donato was nearly in tears as Werner Kuragin – whose given name was Paul Cohen – cooed, 'Ah, caro mio, the public – they are ignorant, the multi-headed swine – but they are also discerning. They know that your Mendelssohn is, is, is ... well, it is *indescribable*! Who has been able to show such depths as you, depths that ascend ever steeper?'

'Depths, depths?' Donato was stupefied. 'You cannot tie me to a warhorse forever!'

Werner was silent for a moment but Donato could hear the shrug.

'A warhorse? The exquisite Mendelssohn is a work of the highest art whose heights can never be fully plumbed. At least that is what I and others far greater than I have believed for many years. I am surprised to hear you speak of this magnificent creation so unjustly.'

A long pause ensued, Donato unable to respond.

'And they will pay for the Mendelssohn like nothing else. The great Paganini whom – yes, I will freely admit in the honesty of my heart and my mother's grave – you alone have surpassed – even he, your countryman, could not display his arsenal. Of course if you wish to cancel so that you may play the *Caprices* Paganini himself would not play in public, I suppose it may be arranged.'

Donato fumed silently, and Werner continued. 'But perhaps the Genovese villa, the apartment on the Seine (what a magnificent view!), the penthouse on Central Park West ... '

Donato pressed his right forefinger onto the touch pad of the sleek web-browsing, music-playing, video-recording, map-displaying, alarm-sounding, logarithmic-calculating contraption, lamenting the days when one could slam a phone down properly on its cradle to make a point. He cinched his silken bathrobe around his growing waist and stepped out onto his balcony, surveying the green teeming Genovese countryside he could hardly enjoy.

It was a sultry summer, a hiatus for the virtuoso. And then an espresso materialised at his elbow as if by magic: there was the beautiful Isabella who started it all!

An hour later he watched the lissome soprano wrap her alabaster neck, the neck on which he had lavished such abundance of kisses, in a heavy woolen scarf. 'It's all I have,' she said meeting his query, and Donato, so cognisant of her unwrapped charms, could not bring himself to dispute. He instead attempted to divulge the – yes, depths! – of his frustration with Werner, with his impossible schedule, with the ceaseless demands made upon him by his instrument and his audience, and with his thwarted artistry. However Isabella's upcoming debut at La Scala rendered her perceptual apparatus as impervious to others' woes as a skydiver's on a descent. She had to hurry, as usual, and when Donato reached around to embrace her in parting he grazed the fourth finger of his left hand (laymen would call the pinky the fifth finger, but, alas, violinists have their own code) against the stone balustrade of his garden path. It smarted and throbbed as Isabella sped away in her embarrassingly yellow Fiat coupé.

* * *

Donato had not yet begun to re-establish the strenuous practice regimen that had preceded each of the past dozen concert seasons. Typically within the month he would reclaim his Guarnerius and build himself up gradually into playing shape, so that by late September he could re-enter the fray. He flexed his pinky which seemed still a bit sore.

As he walked within his garden at twilight, whose magnificent flowerings gave little solace to the disconcerted musician, he strangely mused. What if in the course of going about his ordinary business something should happen to his left hand? Regarding the concern his lover had for her far less valuable throat, he was seized by panic. What if that hand, the hand that could play so exquisitely, the hand responsible for such an ineffable vibrato, the hand for which the accursed but necessary public paid so handsomely (a good pun, but not entirely humourous), what if this treasured instrument of talent were hurt? What if, by dint of even a trifling accident, his schedule were disrupted because of injury? Conductors and agents loathed disruptions. And what if an injury were to endure? His livelihood, his legacy, his *rents* – were they not wholly and utterly dependent upon the health of that marvellous appendage Lucian Freud had so often begged him to depict?

He hurriedly retrieved a glove from his wardrobe. For a while this allayed his fears, though he took care to use the hand gingerly. At the market in the piazza, for example, he relied solely upon his right to assess the summer fruits before purchase. He decided not to remove the glove during the night lest he inadvertently shift in his sleep.

With each passing day the peril into which his unthinking habits had placed him for so many years before became terrifyingly apparent. How could he have so blithely ignored the omnipresent risks that incessantly threatened? Only the grace of a god he could not bring himself to trust had left him unscathed thus far.

And then it dawned upon Donato that his right hand was equally in jeopardy! After all, the hand whose supple strength guided the bow was every bit as necessary as the other. How could he have been so foolish not to have understood this before? He fetched the glove's fellow and now, except for washing, kept both hands protected day and night.

Donato called to his manservant. 'Giuseppe, kindly procure for me from the library these books of anatomy.' When Giuseppe diligently returned with a stack of tomes Donato immersed himself in their content. He learned about the flexor digitorum profundus and the abductor pollicis brevis, among other things. How intricate were the muscles of the hand! And how vulnerable were the distal phalanges! The opportunities for trauma seemed, like the possibilities of artistic expression, infinite.

After he had attained a knowledge of hand anatomy to rival a surgeon's Donato decided to accompany Giuseppe to the library to return his books. An elderly woman was making her way out of the building and unwittingly ground the tip of her cane into Donato's foot. This caused yet another and far more profound epiphany, for it was only then that Donato finally understood the inextricable link between the rest of his body and his hands. From that day on he remained at home.

Soon however it would be time to take up the fiddle and resume preparations for practice. But as Donato thought of the risk not only from the thousands of digital impacts but also from the inevitable flexing of his wrists and elbows, not to mention the rotation of his right shoulder, he demurred.

When Werner visited he was aghast to find the musician resting immobile on a chaise, no evidence of musical initiative in sight. Isabella, whose sensibility could not accept a gloved amorous encounter, had long left for Milan. Only Donato's mother approved, as his new-found mania for safety brought her son closer. He now allowed her full access to his home, whereas before, like an ingrate, he had demanded a modicum of privacy. She shuddered at his goings on with the *puttane* he called his girlfriends.

'I am practicing mentally,' Donato replied to Werner's entreaties.

'That is wonderful, no doubt, and I applaud it,' said the ever-tactful manager, 'but there is something to be said about the physical, is there not?' Werner smiled in that vacant, ter-rified way one smiles when one is about to lose the source of one's income. 'He needs to rest!' protested Donato's mother. But even she, recognising at length the consequences of her son's prolonged inertia, began to become frantic. His good for nothing father, an ignorant banker of all things whose salary was a pittance, relatively speaking, would never be able to keep her in the manner to which she had become accustomed by her son's largesse, now in jeopardy.

When Donato confided in her that he had also aban-doned mental practice once he had divined that impulses arising from within the mind could affect the peripheral nerves, she fainted.

Nonetheless, she and Werner, after long consultation, decided on a plan. Werner prided himself on his psycho-logical acumen and Donato's mother on her intuition, and together they hatched a desperate scheme. In a trattoria on the outskirts of Genoa's centre a young woman, quite plain in looks, played viola with accordion accompaniment. She was notorious for the rough way in which she handled the pitiable instrument, as Werner had discovered one night after a jaunt to a neighbouring establishment. When he saw how she massacred the strings, fingerboard and even the bow with her chubby inelegant fingers, the idea was born: once Donato himself perceived that such violence was harmless, he would be shaken out of the doldrums.

The violinist was entering a phase wherein he wondered about the damage created by music to the auditory apparatus and thence to the higher cortical functions. He no longer attended musical events, as was his wont in summertime, nor did he tolerate the radio or even recordings at home. He had begun, ominously, to complain about the birds. However out of a sense of duty to his mother, he agreed to allow the violist and her accompanist to give a brief performance in the garden.

The girl was dressed garishly in purple and gold and though thrilled to be playing for such a famous artist showed not the least bit of apprehension. Her accordionist, a weather-beaten and wizened old codger, smiled toothlessly. Donato regarded them both with dispassionate detachment at first, but as they moved through their folk staples, he found himself curiously stirred. The songs of his land, of the Mediterranean, of ripening grapes, of fetching women and lazy sunburnt men, of impossible loves, and of that *dolce far niente* that made such contrast to his current state ... Donato sat up and leaned forward. He rose as if in trance after they rendered Tosti's "Marechiare" (quite sloppily, mind you, but with verve) and reached out for the girl's hands. How they had blasted the overgrown fiddle, and yet how beautiful they seemed. She blushed deeply as he turned them over, inspecting the pads and tips of her fingers scrupulously and incredulously. After several moments Donato brought them to his lips, each and every one.

By the time he kissed the fourth finger of her playing hand – the pinky! – she could contain herself no longer. She grabbed Donato's head by the ears and devoured his lips with her own. His mother screamed but Werner led her aside as the girl ripped the violinist's clothes off, beginning with his gloves.

Donato did not play the Mendelssohn Concerto again. Instead of resuming his concert career he formed a quartet with the violist, whom he married. They travelled throughout Italy, and he frequently performed compositions for unaccompanied violin on the second half of an evening's programme, delighting especially in the ricochet bowings and descending scales in thirds of his devilish fellow-countryman.

Violin Caprice No. 2

Mandy O'Callaghan practiced law for the firm Montgomery, Epstein, Roberts, DiDonato and Ellery and most of her work, which she prosecuted with the tenacity of a starved terrier, consisted of defending the huge financial institutions involved in mortgage-lending to the ignorant and poor. *Caveat emptor* was her self-soothing motto. Both she and her husband, a managing partner, did well, very well. In five years, barring another calamity in the Market, they would be able to retire to one of their three homes with an interest income of 3.7 – 4.3 million dollars per annum. They weren't the Rockefellers, but they could live comfortably.

Mandy was also a beauty and this obvious fact lent her spouse, ten years her senior and long past hope of eliminating a gut that preceded the rest of him like an advance brigade, a certain enviable status, though behind closed bedroom doors his marital pleasures only occasionally trespassed the visual. Mandy was tall with stunning shoulder-length red hair and green vixen eyes. She could scorn breast-enhancement because of her natural attributes and kept herself extremely slender by eating virtually nothing and exercising ferociously. Pregnancy was initially traumatic but thankfully within six months of giving birth she had shed all but two and a half pounds of her childbearing weight.

Now, five years later, she was still a pound or two over her ideal no matter how hard she worked out. The all-protein diet in fashion had made her sick so she resigned herself to the extra baggage, discernible to no eye other than her own – and to the scales, of course – with magisterial magnanimity. It was the price, or rather the gift, of motherhood. Her career had hardly been nudged by the pregnancy, for she managed to get to the office two weeks before the arrival of her child, and to return a month afterwards thanks to the hired hands at home. The time she spent with her beautiful daughter, though perhaps not long as conventionally measured by the clock, was invariably cheerful and of the highest quality.

Pre-school had already begun and the four-year old Marcia was the star of her class, able to read seven grades ahead of her age level and obeying her teachers in all things great and small. At the year's first fundraiser, however, a newly arrived classmate opened the festivities by playing a miniature violin. Mandy and all the other mothers (and, to be sure, the few fathers that attended) gasped as the little girl in the rumpled dress showed a technical command and ability to make music that astonished and incited anxious envy. Shortly thereafter nearly all of the children were enrolled in a Suzuki programme. The headmistress was exceedingly pleased as this would cement the reputation of the pre-school as the region's nonpareil, attract even heftier donations and allow her to raise tuition without a murmur.

Marcia enjoyed the novelty of the small violin she was given and she glowed in the devotion she received from her mother every night after dinner. To Mandy's delight she made quick progress: "Twinkle, Twinkle" was already a work of art! But Marcia's attention began to waver. 'Mommy, can I play with Susie now?' asked the girl before they began an evening's session. 'You can play with Susie only after you've finished going through your variations,' replied the mother. Although Marcia was sick to death of "Twinkle, Twinkle" she twinkled on for her reward, the half-hour of playtime with her best friend and neighbour before bed. Thankfully at her enlightened school homework of any kind had been banned: ACTIVE LEARNING HAPPENS HERE! was blazoned across the entranceway to the classroom. Mr. Suzuki's approach seemed different, from what Mandy could tell, as he insisted on daily and rigourous practice no matter what.

A month later Marcia staged a strike. When Mandy entered her room the child was sitting with arms and legs folded, her mouth in a dramatic pout. The small violin was nowhere to be found. Mandy cajoled, teased, enticed and, finally, threatened, but all to no avail. Marcia's lower lip protruded more prominently and tears welled in her eyes, but she would not budge. 'Maybe the kid needs a night off,' suggested the father. Mandy sent him away with a withering gaze that dissolved any amatory illusions for the rest of the year.

Unable to bear the sight of her daughter's now-quivering lower lip, Mandy hit upon an idea. She hugged the child, stroked her adorable red locks, and asked how she would feel if she, her mom, took up the fiddle so they could play together. The exhausted young thing sobbed in her mother's breast and then jumped up, twirled several times around her room ('Be careful, sweetie!' urged the relieved Mandy), and ran to tell her dad the good news.

For a while the arrangement worked splendidly. Marcia delighted in her natural superiority to Mandy's awkward attempts to play on the full-size violin a dealer had been able to sell her for a mere $35,000, which was at virtually no profit to himself, so happy was he to help the cause of music. 'You can barely buy a cigar-box for anything less,' said the avuncular Italian. 'Better to start off with pride!' he added.

Soon enough troubles began anew. Spring had arrived and Marcia longed to go outside. Her father had taught her to throw a ball like a boy and she impressed her schoolmates with the speed of her delivery. Jonathan, who sat at her table, cried out when he hurt his hand catching her during recess, and had to be sent home early.

Mandy threw in the towel. It was clear that Marcia's new talent had eclipsed the girl prodigy's, whose debut had faded away like an irrelevant objection in a courtroom. At the school's Spring Carnival she was trotted out to throw bullets at the not-so-happy Board Chairman who was traditionally the "clown in a cage" perched above a vat of water. Whereas most years two or three lucky strikes from the cherubs would land him in the soup, on this day after Marcia's twenty-fourth unerring pitch he called it quits. She was bought off with a stuffed elephant thrice her size.

Some time had passed, the violins all but forgotten, when Mandy returned home from yet another successful defense of exquisitely calculated financial exploitation. She retrieved her instrument, admitting to herself that unlike everything else she had attempted, this would not come easy. Getting into an Ivy League law school, clerking with powerful judges, passing the Bar, obtaining a post at one of the most prestigious firms on the East Coast, marrying a smart and wealthy man who wouldn't pester her overmuch – these had been, for her, elementary. The violin, however, was something apart.

She had always believed in beginning at the beginning so, like her daughter, she started with Suzuki Book One. It was hardly a picnic. No matter how hard she tried she was never quite in tune. Taking to heart the master's instructions not to proceed until having perfected a piece, she could never move beyond "Twinkle, Twinkle." Despite listening assiduously to the recording and playing along with it repeatedly, somehow or other she just couldn't achieve either acceptably accurate intonation or rhythm. Nevertheless, she persisted. For hours after dinner her daughter and husband would hear nothing but a thin scraping out of the tune she could not transcend.

At work, where it was routine for employees to have their web visits audited, she was discovered to have been spending 73% of her logged-in time on violin blogs or watching various Youtube clips of ancient and sundry violinists. Her husband's prominence at the firm prevented action, but she was beginning to develop a reputation.

She read about the history of fiddling and fiddle-making in an effort to uncover a secret that might allow her to sound a beautiful note. She attended every concert involving stringed instruments within a radius of 90 miles. Imperceptibly she grew heavier, which made her all the more voluptuously alluring.

'Hey, honey,' said her husband one evening in bed, 'have you thought about picking up the guitar instead?' She left his side immediately and began sleeping in the guest room. Within several weeks she made the separation official by moving to her own apartment. Marcia, surprisingly enough, enjoyed the new arrangement, receiving more attention individually from each parent than when they had lived together.

One day while at the luthier's, just as the very same Italian who had sold Mandy her first fiddle had convinced her, for the sake of tone, to purchase a far older and more expensive one, a burly bearded man entered. He removed a violin from its battered hard case. It was old and beaten, with patches of worn varnish splotching its belly. 'I think it's time for a new bridge,' he bellowed genially. Mandy shuddered, turning her back on him.

But then the stranger, oblivious to her and to the violin-maker, began to play a tune. It reminded her of wild and beautiful gypsies on a heath round a fire. His tone was round and solid and resonant and when he came to the end of the brief song she felt her knees buckle. Her mouth opened, parting her lips, and closed again with a sigh.

It didn't take long for them to make a home together while eschewing the institution of marriage. He was an anarchist who taught history at the local community college and his clear and kind explication of the struggles of the working class inspired her to transfer her legal talents, albeit at an unthinkable reduction in salary, to the American Civil Liberties Union. He also taught her how to get beyond "Twinkle, Twinkle" on the violin so that after a year not only was she nearing the completion of Suzuki Book One, but she was also performing a few hearty folk songs in duet, intonation be damned. Marcia had to be torn away from them when it was time for her to stay with her father who by now had married his gorgeous secretary. It wasn't that she didn't like the new woman who made her dad pretty happy, it was just that she wasn't nearly as much fun as her real mom had finally become.

Violin Caprice No. 3

What really irked was knowing that were an illness to disable or an injury hobble him, or were he to be hit by a truck crossing the street, say, to Symphony Hall, the public reaction would be far less horrified than when he was the *enfant terrible* of the violin some forty years before. Now, well, how much fantasied potential could there be to lament?

Gustavo looked carefully both ways before attempting the intersection with his Stradivarius, the 1690 "Medici," musing about Fate and fates. What he had expected to be a brief respite from the concert circuit, shocking as it was then to the musical establishment, had turned into an eternity. Not necessarily a bad one, mind you, but, well, he had been lionised as a youth at a time when musical acrobatics outweighed musical wisdom and now, except for the odd appearance as soloist with his own orchestra – why did they force those horrid contemporary pieces upon him, pieces that elicited the merest smattering of perfunctory applause? – the daily aggravations of his role as concertmaster had taken their toll. He compiled a very detailed list of these unpleasantnesses, which could be grouped into three categories of ascending vexation: 1) his orchestral colleagues, 2) conductors, and 3) soloists, particularly of the violin.

The Brahms Concerto – for him *the* Concerto, Beethoven be damned – was coming up and the orchestra had engaged a nine-year-old boy, a boy technically quite talented, despite his modern cream-cheese vibrato, but *a mere boy* nonetheless! What could he really know of Brahms, that towering genius gazing magisterially and wistfully backward in time from his heights, or of the score of the concerto that he himself had practiced and studied endlessly over the years?

The blaring horn of a taxi that passed within inches drove away any incipient self-pity as he scurried befuddled against the light towards home. His wife, bless her, generally put him to rights and although she was tone-deaf and had no formal understanding of the realm in which he lived and breathed, she knew what was most essential to a musician: praise, praise, praise! This she had heaped upon him – not that he didn't deserve it, mind you – and Gustavo was genuinely grateful.

Whereas critics and friends ascribed his relinquishment of a solo career either to fear or to the desire to work with one of the greatest conductors to have wielded a baton (now deceased), he realised in his heart that it was mainly because he was a homebody. Incessant travel bored and annoyed him, and when he met Joan, who brought to him relatively boundless love and also wonderful domestic talents, he took the opportunity to settle down and stay in one place. Yes, there were occasional tours, but these were rare and consequently invigorating. Fortunately none of their children, fully grown – or, more accurately, legally adult – were musicians or botanists like their parents. By the time the youngest had arrived Gustavo had forsaken any attempt to introduce the violin or piano, scarred as he was from battles with her predecessors (though there still might be time for her to become a violist,

he sneered). Retail, the hospitality industry, corporate law –
Gustavo swallowed his scorn as he thought of their chosen
paths. Yet the kids all seemed quite happy and were in truth
quite loving, which was saying something. Not that they
would ever be able to appreciate their father's artistry – not
that anyone really could, for that matter.

Joan greeted him with the usual hearty kiss and hug and
then a message from the orchestra's manager, Joel, a thirty-
something with a degree, can you imagine, in *orchestra
administration* (when did they start calling this education?).

'I suppose he wants me to play another children's concert,
which I will refuse,' he muttered.

The thought of hordes of noisy, ignorant and smelly children herded by their schoolteachers like unwilling rodents
and accompanied by legions of anxious mothers wishing to
have their precious progeny inoculated with "culture"; of the
bassoon's "hilarious" animal sounds; of the balloons; of the
clowns cavorting to Mozart's minuets....

'Gustavo, hi, this is Joel.'

'I won't do it, forget about it.'

'What? What are you talking about?'

'You know what I'm talking about. I've had enough of
these goddamned kids' concerts, get someone else. You can
talk to our union rep if you don't like it.'

He hung up. The phone rang again within seconds.

'I told you already and I won't change my mind!' shouted
Gustavo.

'No, wait!' screeched Joel. 'Hold on there, it's not what
you think, it's about the Gala, the Brahms and Beethoven:
we need you.' Joel's accent on the second syllable of the latter
composer's name grated like a trumpeter's flubbed note.

'Of course you need me for the Brahms and the *Bee*thoven,' replied Gustavo, emphasising the correct pronunciation, 'I'm the concertmaster, in case you've forgotten, and anyway, who else in the section can play in tune?'

'No, look, be serious for a minute, please, and hear me out. We need you to solo. In the Brahms.'

A long pause.

'Gustavo, don't hang up, are you there?'

'What happened to the troll? Did he get the mumps?'

'No, actually children are vaccinated nowadays and they don't get the mumps anymore, or the measles for that matter.'

'So you're a doctor now?'

'No, Gustavo, be reasonable. I thought you would be *ecstatic* at the opportunity.'

'Ecstasy is for the young, Joel, and the deluded. I'm a realist. Now tell me what happened to the wunderkind.'

'I'm not absolutely certain,' answered Joel conspiratorially, 'but it looks like he's in a Mexican standoff with his mother. For the past two weeks he's refused to touch the violin and now she's called off the concert – she's also his manager, by the way – because she's afraid he won't be up to speed and, well, you know, one poor showing would risk ruining his career.'

'You mean *her* career, don't you?'

Joel laughed.

'What does Andre say?' Andre, Joel's partner and a contract percussionist, knew every imaginable bit of gossip in the immense but small world of classical music. Joel coughed and then qualified his forthcoming remarks as 'not gospel.'

'Andre says the kid developed a crush on his twenty-two year old French tutor, who is rumoured to be quite a hottie. The mother threw her out after she found her massaging his right shoulder, which was apparently not in the lesson plan. It seems pretty innocent to me, but you know how mothers are, don't you? So Dmitri staged a protest.'

'Good for him! The kid's got spunk. Like Heifetz said, child prodigism is a disease that's usually fatal. Maybe he'll survive.'

'Good old Jascha!' chirped Joel.

'*Jascha*, what do you mean, *Jascha*?' cried Gustavo. 'You're still in diapers, Joel, but you're on a first name basis with Heifetz? Unless you're already a damned good violinist yourself you can't even imagine just how phenomenal he was. I bet you don't own even *one* of his records, do you? Go ahead, tell the truth!' he continued hotly.

'Yes, in fact I do, Gustavo, so will you relax, *please*?'

Any mention of Heifetz by anyone, himself included, favourable or unfavourable, generally acted like an irritant, for Gustavo was well aware that Oistrakh was entirely correct when he said, 'There are violinists. And then there's Heifetz.' Therefore the concertmaster relented.

'But what about the others? Why me?'

'Everyone, and I mean *everyone*, respects your virtuosity, Gustavo.'

'Cut it out, Joel. What happened to the ten-year-old Korean girl?'

'She's in Australia. And the A-list are all engaged.'

'Both of them? Gee, my heart goes out.' And in truth there were hardly a dozen violinists whom the orchestra would deign to invite, none of which was free. How could they be? To keep their place in the rotation they couldn't afford a week off from the schedules that had been prearranged for them five years in advance.

'Gustavo, it's our last concert of the season, our gala, our fundraiser, the house will be full, the entire Board will be there, everybody loves *Bee*thoven and Brahms and ... and people still remember you, the people who matter.' He paused for a moment. 'We need you.'

We need you. Gustavo was even tempted to believe that Joel was sincere.

'Alright,' he replied laconically, before adding as an after-thought, 'How's Tomás about it?' Tomás, the musical direc-tor and one of the few conductors who studied scores as assiduously as did Gustavo, was a real musician, someone from whom, he grudgingly confessed, he occasionally learned something. Tomás, however, was also handsome, relatively young, impeccably tailored, meticulously coiffed and delib-erately unmarried, which made for a bit of resentment. He kept the orchestra afloat by attracting serious money from elderly benefactresses who appreciated his tailoring, groom-ing and ostentatious athleticism on the podium; being par-tially deaf they had a more difficult time judging the merits of his music.

'C'mon, whose idea do you think it was anyway, mine?' cackled Joel. 'I'll let them know right away. Thanks a million, Gustavo, oh, and one last question.'

Gustavo waited.

'I don't mean to, well, Gustavo,' Joel stuttered, 'since the first performance is just two weeks away, do you think you will, that it, that, like, you know, that you'll have it, like,' he concluded, nearly inaudibly, 'ready?'

Gustavo slammed down the handset of his antiquated and therefore immobile phone and Joel was wise enough not to call again.

* * *

For a moment Gustavo experienced sheer terror, the kind that his stand-partner, a young woman far too pretty for her own good, must have suffered when she discovered Gary Larson cartoons plastered over the final movement of Schumann's *Fourth* during a concert a few months back. He of course could play the part from memory, in his sleep or while eating a soft pretzel, but she on the other hand, newly hired ...

Then he got to work, with relish, allowing himself finally to feel fully the great good fortune of this unexpected opportunity to – to achieve vindication, victory, revenge? Yes, scoundrel that I am, he thought, I want those things. However his wife's unabashed joy on his behalf quickly relegated such pettiness to the outer crusts of his soul, so that his genuine desire to commune with and express the truths and beauties of an incomparable creation flourished.

Although he was convinced that over the many years of his tenure his virtuosic technique had actually improved, he had grave apprehensions about the final movement of the concerto, which Tomás was known to take at a breakneck pace. When he confessed such misgivings to Joan she grew pensive. The day before rehearsals she produced a tea derived from Amazonian herbs described by the ethnobotanist Richard Schultes, a drink used by the wives of tribal warriors on the eve of battle, when they were compelled by their gods to weave new ornamental headgear for their spouses between dusk and dawn, a challenge that required dexterity like lightning. Gustavo was skeptical but he drank the potion, which tasted, he thought, a bit like chamomile and honey.

But boy did it work! At rehearsal he felt strangely elated and energised, negotiating the concerto with such deftness of touch and in the last movement such dancing gossamer speed that Tomás raised an eyebrow and members of the orchestra tapped their bows and stamped their feet in admiration and approval, causing him no little embarrassment and delight. Joan cautiously limited his intake of the brew to two cups daily. Gustavo could hardly believe his fingers were capable of such agility. If only he had known about this years before!

The great night arrived and Gustavo made his entrance onstage with Tomás, calm and confident as a lion. Then they were off! Everything went splendidly. His colleagues accompanied gorgeously and Tomás was working up a healthy sweat that threatened to dislodge a hair or two. The standing ovation was stentorian and, more important, deserved, for Gustavo knew he had achieved something wonderful when he had found his way to a number of spontaneous surprises in the expression of that glorious score.

Joel hurried to congratulate him backstage during the intermission and then earnestly took him aside.

'Okay, I'll play for the kids,' bantered the smiling soloist.

Joel was uncharacteristically ruffled and, for a youngster, even solemn.

'Tomás is not feeling well – the doctor checked him out and it's not his heart, thank goodness. But he can't go on. He thinks it was the raw clams he had for dinner. He wants you to take the baton for the *Seventh*.'

And so Gustavo compounded his triumph that evening, helped in no small measure by his scandalous encore of Beethoven's sublimely Bacchic Allegro (which is what orchestras did in Beethoven's day, and besides, the entire concert fell well within the two hours allotted by the musicians union!). Critics, music lovers and the Board were, for once, unanimous in unadulterated astonished appreciation.

Thus began for the violinist a new, albeit part-time, career on the podium, at an age when such gifts come rarely.

A year later at dinner with Joan, Tomás and Tomás' chic new girlfriend (an artist turned stockbroker) in Prague, where he had been invited to guest conduct, Gustavo learned that his wife's concoction was not from the Amazon and that Tomás had never eaten a clam in his life.

Violin Caprice No. 4

'The kid's good, Marty, but it's not enough.'

'Tell me about it.'

Miguel Jackson was having another very good round at the gym, light on his feet and deft with his counter-punching, while his trainer and manager looked on.

'Good isn't enough these days,' sighed Marty, pot-bellied and wrinkled, reeking of cigar. 'You gotta be an entertainer, you gotta have a catch.'

The diminutive Vinnie, whose canny eyes missed nothing in the ring while they spoke, nodded.

'That's your department. I can get him to the big time on skill, which he's got plenty of, and with heart to boot, but it ain't enough. Think of something.'

'That's all I do is think, but how do you sell a Black Hispanic or Hispanic Black, whatever the hell he is, of which there are only a few hundred million in the game? He's a marketing nightmare, Vinnie, the kid's a loner, he's quiet, he's got no tattoos, no posse, and he's not exactly a knockout artist.'

Vinnie protested. 'He's twenty-three and one, and eighteen *are* TKOs, which are knockouts.'

'That's not the same.'

'How can I help it if they stop the fights before it gets to that stage? He's a damned good boxer, Marty. He's pure, if you know what I mean, like Willie Pep.' Vinnie sighed remembering the days when a fighter could just fight, when all he had to do was win either by outsmarting, outpunching or outboxing an opponent fair and square, barring of course the usual fixes. Now, you needed an angle, a moniker, a stage routine to get to the big show, otherwise promoters weren't interested, no matter what your record.

'We're on the same page, Vinnie, I'm just telling you reality. It'd be a lot easier if he were a Chinese-Jew with a retarded brother dying from leukaemia – at least there'd be a story line for the press. He doesn't even have a goddamned nickname.'

'Think of something, Marty, help us out. Hell, I'm already up there and he won't stay in the game for peanuts. He's a good kid – doesn't do dope, doesn't drink, doesn't whore around, and he's a helluva boxer. Look at him.'

They watched while he effortlessly avoided a huge left hook and countered over top with a right – Miguel was a southpaw – sending his sparring partner to the canvas.

Marty frowned because he was stymied, but he winked at Miguel who waved his gloves in return as the round ended. The lithe muscular young man leaned over the ropes for Vinnie's advice.

Two weeks later Marty burst into Vinnie's gym wearing a smile as broad as his midsection. He'd scored a coup: the undercard of a light-heavyweight title bout at the Garden. Big time audience, decent money, pay-per-view, and Eddie "The Avalanche" Jones, a former champion on the comeback trail. Nine months away.

Vinnie salivated. The "Avalanche" was perfect. In his hey-day Eddie Jones was a murderer, cutting off the ring and devas-tating opponents with ferocious body punches that brought their arms down and set them up for his trademark combina-tion hook-uppercut to the head, an inevitable knockout. His big mistake – apart from the booze and the girls – was to fight above weight. Now, needing money – and who didn't need money? – even at age thirty-six he would be dangerous. But his style was tailor-made to Miguel's strengths. First, the left hook would be nullified by Miguel's offputting southpaw jab, second, Miguel could outdance an older Eddie and elude the heavy artillery, third, Eddie kept his right hand down out of habit, a very bad habit, and Miguel's left would have an avenue as wide as Broadway to the Avalanche's chin, which was Eddie's Achilles heel, so to speak, not that Vinnie was perturbed by mangled metaphors. Beating Eddie meant that Miguel would be a contender and that he, Vinnie, would get a good piece of change for retirement even if the kid didn't make it all the way to the top. Unless, god forbid, Miguel did something uncharacteristically stupid in the ring, always a possibility when punches were flying, he would be giving the audience at Madison Square Garden a clinic.

'And guess what,' continued Marty with a self-satisfied grin, 'I got us an angle.'

* * *

Miguel had never been further south than Atlantic City and now here he was a few hours from Nashville surrounded by country – *real* country, not a city park – spreading out in every direction.

For a kid who grew up in the North Philly projects the immensity of it all, the lushness of the vegetation and scent, the din of creature sounds and the loneliness were as bewildering as the easy generosity of the locals with their lazy drawls and genial smiles. But he adapted.

He began each morning with a six mile trail run at dawn through the forested hills bordering the Smoky Mountains. Then he was free until his sparring and gym work at three at a make-shift training facility organised by Marty thirty miles away. By six he was back at the shack owned by Marty's nephew, Irving, a studio musician and bluegrass fiddler who had inspired the brainstorm.

At the first publicity stunt Marty orchestrated for the "Fightin' Fiddler" Miguel stood awkwardly onstage with Irving's bandmates, drenched in sweat and clutching a violin whose strings had been greased so as to be noiseless while Miguel sawed away with the bow. Irving himself sat out of view in the wings with an amped fiddle to make it sound real. Miguel's capacious cowboy hat drifted over his eyebrows through the mercifully brief ordeal. As far as news bites go, however, it was a smash. The local stations picked it up, having nothing much else to chronicle, and fed the bizarre clip to their national affiliates who broadcast the image of the up and coming pugilist working a fiddle like a manic Kenny Baker with a bunch of pale-faced hillbillies. Fifteen seconds of notoriety. Marty was thrilled. Mainstream audiences and hard-core boxing fans would respond to the racial overtones and, let's face it, he thought, that's always been a big part of boxing's appeal.

Afterwards Miguel was furious and refused any further charades. Marty and Vinnie begged and wheedled, but it was Irving who saved the day, offering to teach the kid a few licks so he could seem legit next time round. Miguel thought it over and agreed: what the hell, he had three months of nothing else to do ahead of the fight of his life.

'He could have been in the Philly Orchestra,' grumbled Marty to anyone within earshot, 'if only he'd hadda listened to me instead of his *meshugge* father. A Curtis grad, but he gets involved with a cornfed *shiksa*. Klezmer at least I could understand.'

'Give him a break, Marty, he looks like he's happy,' retorted Vinnie.

'Happy? What's happy got to do with it?' But Marty was not so secretly proud of his errant nephew, especially since Irving was helping him out big time, which is what nephews should do anyway for their elders.

Miguel had never touched a musical instrument before in his life until that summer. The fiddle was cumbersomely dwarfed by his large left hand and impossible to balance at first. Irving patiently showed him how he could just turn his head and let its weight fall gently onto the chinrest while the curved back of the violin nestled against his collar bone.

'There,' said Irving, 'no hands.' And indeed Miguel could allow his arm to drop while the fiddle remained poised in place.

Their goals were modest: thirty seconds of something vaguely resembling a country riff for the next and final choreographed appearance one month prior to the bout, and that would be it. Miguel was strangely galvanised by the challenge and within a few weeks he could sound a decent note on each of the strings with his forefinger. Soon he was playing a scale in first position. His being a southpaw provided a musical as well as a pugilistic advantage.

At Irving's cabin there was no radio, no TV, no internet and no car – just Vinnie for company, which wasn't much because he generally nodded out after dinner. Aside from desultory strolls in the countryside dodging mosquitoes, there was very little for Miguel to do except mess about with the fiddle. And so he did, marvelling one night at an unanticipated string of several notes that made him feel – well, he couldn't exactly describe it, but he memorised his fingering and couldn't wait to show Irving.

'That's the blues,' said the fiddler after Miguel demonstrated for him.

'What's the blues?' replied Miguel.

'Just what you did.'

'I kinda like it,' said Miguel bashfully.

Irving smiled. 'So do a lot of people. Look, why don't you come and hear us on Saturday night? Sunday's your day off. Keep a low profile, no drinking, and no messing around, otherwise Marty would kill me.'

On Saturday afternoon they drove down to Nashville and Miguel just couldn't get enough of the bluegrass sound, the cheery crowd and the hospitality of folks united in their love for a music that made you feel good to be alive and not angry. When a Southern belle asked him to dance he fought against every instinct in his humming body to demur.

'Good call,' said Irving afterwards, as Miguel lent a hand with the equipment.

Somehow Marty had learned of the expedition and hit the roof, so that was the end of that. But the excitement lingered and during the long lonesome evenings with the fiddle at hand as the trees rustled outside and unseen insects buzzed and fluttered, as the very earth seemed to swell and breathe around him, he began to think a little more, and to feel, and although he couldn't really find his way to any decision aside from preparing for the fight and making some ready money, the opaque impenetrable wall that had always been the future for him began to give way.

At his next and final gig there were no greased strings and no hidden proxies. For each song of the set Irving had taught Miguel to play one of three notes, nice and easy, while the other fiddlers took off. Then when they covered Bill Monroe's "Rocky Road Blues" Miguel had his solo – a simplified version of Chubby Wise's riff from the original recording, which Miguel executed fairly cleanly, given that they had slowed the tempo considerably. He was elated, the news folk ate it up and the Avalanche and his crew licked their lips in anticipation.

* * *

By round four Miguel had mastered his prey: the Avalanche had thrown his entire aging arsenal at him and had managed to land only a few body blows. He was now swinging wildly and tiring, and when Miguel countered with a strong left uppercut the Avalanche went down. Eddie's eyes were swollen but the cagey fighter had gotten himself up off the canvas and then clinched and mauled his way through the rest of the round. Miguel's left hand throbbed – so much for the Achilles chin, he thought.

'Go for the knockout,' said Vinnie working his corner. Miguel shrugged, ignorant that a substantial bet had been placed on the Avalanche and that anything short of an outright knockout would be defeat.

He continued to jab and dance and to befuddle the Avalanche, but his left hand, which he could barely use in defence, hurt like hell and he knew something was terribly wrong. He could try to keep Eddie off balance for the remainder of the bout with his right, praying for a win on points, having already amassed a sizeable lead, but Vinnie's uncharacteristic request was ominous. Besides, the Avalanche would sniff out his weakness soon enough and force him to go for the KO with his already mangled left, which meant he could kiss the violin goodbye. How else could he nail the cagey bastard? It was either that or throw in the towel. Talk about the blues!

Eddie launched another haymaker that just barely missed its target thanks to a deft but horrifically painful parry from Miguel's wasted hand, and during the ensuing clinch whispered in his opponent's ear.

Both Vinnie and Marty were shocked when, after the break, their fighter whipped a right hook over the Avalanche's left shoulder and then – and this they couldn't believe, it was so damned fast – brought it back in time to move in with a right uppercut that floored the veteran for good.

In the dressing-room afterwards Miguel's left wrist and hand were hugely swollen, and later the doctors confessed he was lucky not to have sustained a severe scaphoid fracture with its attendant risks of chronic pain, avascular necrosis and arthritis. Vinnie and Marty were ecstatically babbling about the title but Miguel was far away in the Smoky Mountains of Tennessee.

He fought once more before hanging up the gloves, making just enough seed money for Vinnie to retire from his cut of the purse and for him to move down South and join Irving as a factotum. His celebrity, tenacity and diligence made him the band's unanimous choice for a manager, which they were sorely in need of, and because his heart was in their music – and because he was a very shrewd negotiator – he helped them to bigger venues and onto the country charts. Irving gave him a damned good fiddle as a token of appreciation, and whenever the time and place were right they cajoled him onstage for his bit in "Rocky Road Blues."

And Miguel never ever heard anyone call him a "fiddlin' fairy" again.

Violin Caprice No. 5

Father Gianpietro Squillace, born to devout immigrant Calabrians in Trenton, New Jersey, began his priestly studies at Saint Charles Borromeo Seminary just outside Philadelphia, a city his parents, like most Jersey residents, visited only when driven by necessity. His proficiency in the finer points of theological dogma was equalled by a passionate fascination with the Lord's work as it was miraculously manifested in human physiology. A three-hundred page dissertation, "Neuroglial Proliferation and Enhanced Synaptic Transmission as a Consequence of Celibacy," earned for him the reward of advanced study at the Vatican, which always welcomed scientific agreement with established articles of faith. After his ordination at Saint Peter's he joined the ecclesiastical ranks that surrounded His Holiness like so many circles of Paradise, rising within a short while to a position of minor but most definite prominence at the Holy See for his erudition and sanctity.

He was accorded great latitude to develop his scholastic talents and, being surrounded by the glories of Italian art, was one day inspired to look more closely at pictorial representations of the Virgin Mary through time, hypothesising that through His human artistic emissaries the Lord Our Father had bequeathed a hidden record of the intricate subtleties of divine revelation. Having been granted permission to pursue his studies at the Uffizi in Florence, the good priest devoted long days to the chronological inspection of the Virgin's many portraits, taking extraordinarily detailed notes about form, line, colour, perspective and the depiction of facial and manual musculature.

When at last he entered the Sala dei Lippi his books fell from him with a thud and he stood transfixed by what he could only apprehend as Grace made visible. Nothing he had seen heretofore had prepared him for this surging resonant apotheosis of tenderness, beauty, nurturant strength, obedience, resignation, humility, wisdom, anticipatory sorrow and motherly love for the Christ and humankind. He dropped to his knees and made the sign of the cross as tears of joyful exhilaration streamed down his youthful mien.

Had his monograph "The Anatomy of Maternal Godliness as First Divulged in Fra Filippo Lippi's *Madonna and Child with Two Angels*" not included extensive appendices on minute aspects of infant nutrition, Father Squillace might well have spent his days toiling in Rome. Instead, his superiors received the work rather coolly, though many unauthorised copies were distributed and colleagues less brimful of the milk of kindness, human or divine, whispered that perhaps the priest's synapses had been firing a bit too recklessly.

And so Father Squillace was returned to America and given custody of a parish not far from his birthplace with a large but dilapidated church standing in a sea of aluminum-clad rowhomes. The population he served was motley: elderly Italians too poor or tired to flee the arrival of younger Blacks, Hispanics and Asians who now made a majority, complemented by a small but implacable contingent of the Irish.

This undaunted good shepherd approached his work with gusto and in less than a decade his parishioners had tripled and the coffers in Rome began filling again from a source it had long ago discounted. Some credited his lengthy and finely reasoned sermons at Sunday mass, some his boyish good looks, and some his mysterious and therefore scandal-tinged reputation; but most agreed that his goal of calling upon the faithful to restore the once-proud edifice of the church to splendour had rallied the community, reinstated hope, mitigated racial divisions and elicited approval from the all-seeing eye of the Vatican. A large and, to be fair, rather crude fresco depicting the Resurrection, was nearly finished. The artisans he had in his employ were taxed to the utmost by the demands of the medium, but they produced some-thing passably colourful and not terribly displeasing. All that remained was the depiction of two heavenly *putti* gaz-ing down with harps in hand as Jesus appeared resplendent outside His tomb.

Father Squillace chatted amiably with his prize painter Sandro on his way to the confessional, relishing the sim-ple yet felicitous plans for the design of the angels they had devised together and musing about the completion of his latest discourse, provisionally entitled "Celibacy-Induced Thickening of the Pre-Frontal Cortex," when he spied a penitent at the altar rail. He paused, disbelieving his eyes: except for her garb – she was clothed in black – she was the very image of Lippi's *Madonna*. Could this be possible? The slope of her forehead, the gentle curve of her lovely nose, the downcast heavy-lidded eyes, the nearly quivering lips and those exquisitely soft hands joined in prayer.... He took his seat in the dark and She entered.

'Father,' She whispered, 'I have come to make my confession.'

'Yes, my child,' responded the priest with gentleness in his voice and sweat on his brow.

She spoke slowly and tentatively at first, pausing often.

'I lost my husband over a year ago. He was a good man who had bad friends and paid the price. I loved him and I love him still. I live alone and I make just enough at my job to keep going, but I don't do much, Father, except ... '

'Yes, my child?'

'Except think about going to meet him,' She confided, barely audible.

'Ah, is that what you wish to confess?'

'That's just half of it, Father. I'm still young, we didn't have children and I was on the point of ending it all a month ago. I had it all planned, I just couldn't go on, even though I knew it would be a mortal sin. I just couldn't help myself, Father!'

She began to sob quietly.

'But the Lord who sees all sent you a message.'

'Yes, Father, yes, that's exactly what He did!' She exclaimed, albeit still in hushed tones. 'The TV was on and I heard a song, a song played by a violin, and it saved me, it was a lifeline! I threw away the pills – a whole handful of them! – and I felt for the first time since Frankie's death – that's what I called him, Father, but everybody else knew him as Fritz the Mensch, don't ask me why – that I could somehow *live*, that I had *hope*, that Frankie would *want* me to live, wouldn't he?'

'Of course, dear child.'

'But when I heard the violin,' She added cautiously, 'I had thoughts, Father. Terrible thoughts, evil and wicked thoughts. They went away but then I got low again, Father, very low, and I ran out to buy more pills. At the drug store

I saw a CD on the sales rack, a smiling man with a violin, for five bucks, and I bought that instead, go figure! And I listened to it, to the violin, and I was filled with *life* again.' She sighed dolefully. 'But the thoughts came back,' She murmured, adding with anguish, 'And if I don't tell you about them I'll *explode*.'

So She told him about Her thoughts, and She had been right. They were indeed terrible and wicked, for they were the thoughts of a wanton. But She was much relieved by the telling and smiled through Her copious tears when he gave Her the penance of ten rosaries, and Father Squillace felt blessed to have been just and merciful.

The next Friday She returned and Father Squillace was astonished and also dismayed by the variety of Her thoughtful transgressions. Again She left gratefully, though this time he had doubled Her penance. By the third week he understood that She was perilously navigating between the Scylla of suicide and the Charybdis of carnality, risking both body and soul, so he devised a stratagem. First, he would take Her confession on a daily basis, excepting Sundays. Second, he would inquire of Her about the sonorities of the violin and thus seek for a clue to Her sinfulness.

She came dutifully every day. Her florid imagination knew no bounds. Thankfully She interspersed the catalogue of Her ingeniously contrived sins with explanatory biography, and over time Father Squillace came to know this childless non-virginal Madonna as he had never known anyone before.

Once in a fit of righteous sternness he forbade Her altogether to listen to the violin but She grew so morose so suddenly and was so listless and ill-appearing when he saw Her again that he countermanded himself. No, desperate situations required brave measures. Twice a week he visited Her home, as he would a dying member of his flock. She came to depend upon and cherish these visits for the salvation of Her soul and greeted him with his favourite freshly brewed coffee and ricotta cannoli made from scratch (except for the ricotta, that is).

Puzzled that She could be influenced to such a degree by the charlatan of the instrument featured on her original CD, the good father experimented by introducing Her to violinists in his own extensive collection. Listening together he could all the more closely observe Her response and would thus be in a decidedly superior position to minister.

Being chronologically disposed he had begun with currently performing classical artists and journeyed backwards in time. When they entered the territory of Kreisler, She responded with eerie radiance, requesting the favour of being addressed by her Christian name. Father Squillace brought Her fingers to his lips as he took his leave, not unlike a fin de siècle Viennese gentleman.

He spent an agonising night in the garden of self-condemnation, for the terrifying reality that Her carnal desires had reached the point of crisis finally dawned. Yet in the midst of this merciless and sleepless ordeal he conceived a brilliant plan.

Sunday next he commenced his sermon meekly, even hesitantly, extolling the glories of the Lord and the temptations placed in the path of the faithful, the most famous of which being Jesus himself in the desert. He moved more stiffly than usual, and walked with small steps, but his voice rang out with its customary urbane resonance.

'Do you remember, my friends,' intoned Father Squillace, 'that Satan asked Jesus to make bread from the stones of the desert? That he brought Him to the highest point of the Temple of Jerusalem and asked Him to prove his Godhead by hurling Himself from the pinnacle? That he promised our Lord Jesus Christ all the kingdoms of the world in return for worship?'

He paused dramatically, scanning the churchgoers with furrowed brimstone brow.

'These temptations,' he thundered, 'mighty as they seem, were as nothing to *this*!'

Here Father Squillace whipped out from the folds of his cassock a fiddle and held it aloft before the bewildered congregation, at the head of which was She smiling Her sorrowfully beatific smile.

As he held it by the neck prepared to shake and elucidate the manifold evils emanating from so seemingly slight a vessel, his eyes alit upon Her and he helplessly shifted course. He spoke instead of the elegant curves of the violin and traced its purfling with delicacy. He described how the merest caress of the bow would set its strings atremble and that the resulting melodious tones spoke the language of communion. He illustrated by reference to its shape how it signified the Trinity and how too it resembled the most beneficent Mother. His language stunned the church-goers. Just what did he mean by nuts, f-holes and rounded bellies?

The foremost pew was set astir when She swooned.

Next week, at the unveiling of the great fresco that marked the culmination of so many aspirations, Father Squillace was nowhere to be found. Sandro, whose only other talent was for bocce, had followed the priest's instructions faithfully. The parishioners gasped when they saw not harps in the hands of the mischievous *putti*, but – violins. Violins! When did violins ever appear in Heaven?

Years later Father Squillace, cultivating peas in a New Mexican monastery, learned that Beatrice had boldly invited Sandro to her home on the evening of the unveiling of his art. She insisted on playing violin music the entire night, and Sandro didn't mind one bit.

Violin Caprice No. 6

What happened to Kikinski? You will scarcely believe me, but so be it. Listen: I swear to you on the grave of my mother to give you the truth of it all. *Cameriere, un bicchiere di vino, per favore!*

Kikinski was given to wild, exorbitant and dramatic gestures on the podium. It is true indeed, however, that he electrified audiences, and even those cynical and weary musicians who played for him grudgingly admitted that his sense of timing was, well, unnerving. I refer to his uncanny ability to erupt like a veritable volcano and leap into the air, taking the orchestra with him, or to thrust his baton as powerfully and incisively as a *coup de foudre* at preternaturally precise moments of a performance, keeping both players and audiences on edge, and sometimes, breathlessly so. But it was his trademark lavish and singular mane of hair that lent a special galvanic grace and set him apart. Because his hair – well, in the interests of exactitude, it wasn't exactly *his* hair, but I will get to that in a moment – fell to his shoulder blades, there were many possibilities. In quiet rhythmic passages it could swing gently and softly from side to side, and of course in more explosive moments it would uncoil like a whip before fluttering back. As Kikinski's head was never still his golden locks constantly shimmered. The orchestra's marketing advisors took full advantage and the orchestra itself had become virtually synonymous with the halo of Kikinski's dazzling flying curls.

For Kikinski, being vastly bald, keeping up this image had its challenges, challenges he had artfully conquered. He had recognised quite early in his career, as he grunted his way up the narrow ladder to notoriety, that his youthful plumes would soon give way to the smooth shining nothingness of his father and grandfather. All are born bald, all achieve baldness, and some have baldness thrust upon them far too soon; Kikinski was one of these latter. True, for some men baldness was an attribute, a sign of virility, but owing to an irregular and misshapen skull Kikinski could not count on baldness as a blessing. I use strong but accurate words when I say that he positively *feared* it, that he *trembled* before the prospect!

Fate came to his rescue in the form of a very pretty French violinist of the second section – and really, she was an adorable vixen as well as a decent but unremarkable fiddler. In an uncharacteristically forthcoming moment, enchanted by her charms, he confessed his concerns for the future of his looks and, consequently, his career. To his immeasurable surprise, his sagacious lover suggested a remedy that was to prove a masterstroke. She urged him to shave his pate immediately and allow her to construct a wig – a wig that would be indiscernible from his now-flowing locks and that, under the guidance of her deft fingers, would change imperceptibly and appropriately over time. His flourishing fleece would appear to age naturally with him while yet preserving the illusion of endless youth. This of course required great skill, unflagging attention, and a pact of secrecy.

Kikinski, being wary, initially demurred, but when she came to him with an example of her handiwork and set it upon his head, he was completely enthralled. Her delicate fingers tousled and arranged to perfection the curls and strands of the hairpiece while the maestro gazed at the mirror with satisfied acceptance. 'What a good looking fellow,' he thought, 'what an irresistible rogue!'

Mlle. Tesi hailed from a family of beauticians and apothecaries in Provence and in short order not only did Kikinski have his ideal head of hair, he also received, through the generous Frenchwoman, an herbal tincture that cured the insomnia that had dogged him forever and would have aged him beyond his years if unchecked.

As he admired her latest example of artistry one evening in anticipation of a minor event, only local dignitaries, alas, scheduled to be present, she allowed the very tips of her fingers to caress the lobes of his partially obscured ears. This was a sign that she, who in matters of the boudoir was as ceaselessly fascinating as in matters of coiffure, would more than compensate for his frustrated ambition.

Kikinski came to regard Mlle. Tesi as irreplaceable. As he ascended the ranks and forged an illustrious career, he brought her along with him and safely placed her into the midsection of his latest orchestra's second violins where she performed quite competently, if indifferently, and elicited little envy from her more musically ambitious female colleagues. In a moment of weakness he even contemplated marriage to preserve the secret that became more precious with the passing of time – an institutional fortification, as it were. But the knowledge that her own station was firmly in his control, and that her provenance from the lower social orders would make her eternally give thanks for an

association with his noble pedigree and celebrity, kept him
from taking this fatal step. They were in any case married in
all but name, though they lived apart to insulate each other
from the mundane and passion-mitigating demands of the
ordinary. On the several occasions when he was fleetingly
tempted to stray, a simple gaze in the mirror confirmed
her unequalled talents. Risking her loss would amount to
risking the loss of his own ideal, now gazing back at him
enchantingly.

The conductor mused dreamily upon such matters as
his lover's fingers massaged his scalp in preparation for the
application of the fixative that held the talisman in place, a
fixative of her own devising that withstood the most violent
of movements and therefore gave Kikinski complete freedom from worry to cavort and exhort on the podium. He
shook his head and counted his blessings. His dutiful and
adoring acolyte was putting the finishing touches on his own
ravishing mien, inflaming him as not even a Carmen could!

Alas, the inevitable one day transpired – there is always
the inevitable, isn't there?

A very fetching and very fine violinist half Kikinski's age
and two-thirds the age of Mlle. Tesi, had come to town to
perform the *Poème* of Chausson – musically a rather trivial
piece, though not without a certain charm and providing an
opportunity or two for drama. The soloist had, in addition
to a modest curvaceousness, the most lustrous and alluring
auburn hair, hair that nearly rivalled his own for effect: it
magnetised his attention. She was also refreshingly accepting
of his musical suggestions; she hung in fact upon his every
pearl-like utterance, unlike the usual pigheaded brutes who
would acknowledge his direction as if under hardship, arrogant bastards! She, however, while at rehearsal sought out

his recommendations and even requested, if he could spare the time, which was hard to imagine for so busy and important a man as he, a private coaching session.

Somehow Kikinski, to the sly amusement of the orchestra, might just manage an hour or two out of his impossible schedule, for after all, they were servants of Music, were they not? Kikinski's strange ruddiness and a smile that threatened to expose his gumline did not go unnoticed by Mlle. Tesi.

He and the violinist spent the entire afternoon in the blissful explorations of the marvels of Chausson's score, the subtle and beautiful intricacies of the engagement between the violin and orchestra, and the far-reaching metaphorical underpinnings of the composition's palette, agreeing, the both of them, that no other such paean to Love, magnificent, daunting, tender yet all-fulfilling Love, had ever been composed. Had it not been for the maestro's fear that his locks would not survive the natural extension of their inquiries, their discussions would have been singularly deepened that very day. They swore, however, to continue their investigations after the concert.

Kikinski, who was certainly no fool, knew enough of feminine intuition to realise that Mlle. Tesi might suspect something amiss when she arrived to prepare him for the evening's performance. He therefore determined to suppress his burgeoning elation by assuming an attitude of easy (not exaggerated!) nonchalance. He also hit upon a shrewd psychological ploy sure to bury any misgivings: he casually suggested that she tend to the violinist's coiffure, for the poor thing was clearly in need of grooming, *anything* to spruce up that savage mop with which she was afflicted. As she had in past occasionally lent a similar hand to visiting artists, Tesi cheerfully accepted her commission. To know that his current lover would be caressing his lover-to-be gave the clever Kikinski a secret thrill and only added to his already frenzied anticipatory excitement.

Timing is everything, and as I've already told you, Kikinski was a master. He had worked out to perfection his every gesture during the performance of the *Poème*, which would conclude the evening's programme. At first he would be still, allowing his nymphette with her singing instrument to trill and shine amidst the shimmering orchestral textures. Occasionally he would meet her eyes with his own to find her welcoming fire with fire, and as the composition wove its way to the heights, he would become bolder and more demonstrative in his choreography until, at its climactic peak where violin and orchestra surge together in ecstatic intensity moments before the quiet impressionistic ending, he would suddenly whip his head and torso towards her and raise his baton to the heavens.

As Kikinski strode onstage with the violinist it is fair to say that he, with his golden-grey glowing curls, and she, with her magnificent dark tresses bound in a stunning quiff, augmented by an elegant gown with sensational décolletage, seemed king and queen of some fabulous realm. The *Poème* unfolded and she played freely and fluidly, buttressed by the maestro and his minions, and in perfect intonation. The audience was utterly enraptured by this dream-like new world opening before them, but when Kikinski uncoiled they were unprepared.

It wasn't so much the astonishing flight of Jason's fleece from Kikinski's head to the tip of the violinist's bow that led to the uproar, although that was shocking enough, for the bald and exposed conductor with his lumpy pate cut a very poor figure, and the reflexive flick that hurled his wig

onto an unsuspecting concert-goer caused some mild dismay. Imagine, however, the reaction of the beautiful violinist
when *at the exact same moment* a small rodent (some say it
was a gerbil, others a field mouse, some a hamster, and still
others an immature rat – one will, alas, never know) awoke
from its nest atop her head and scampered southwards upon
her to another haven.

In matters of timing, Mlle. Tesi cannot have asked for anything better.

Violin Caprice No. 7

She always dreaded these "impromptu" meetings with him. It wasn't a case of their having grown apart over the years because he hadn't grown one iota, and that was the problem. She had diligently and arduously worked her way to the point where not only was she making a decent living doing the thing she loved, but she and her quartet had begun to attract the kind of muted but consistently sound appreciation that signalled longevity. What with teaching, touring and steady practice, she'd had her hands richly full. On several occasions she nearly felt ready to complement her musical activities with domestic ones, but honestly, where and how could she ever find time for children? Her latest flame, a luthier with ridiculous aspirations to rival the Cremonese, didn't press for anything beyond lustful pleasantries and the hobnobbing that went with classical music's circle of support: corporate leaders with kids who had the money to spend on quality instruments for their precious progeny, few of whom would ever touch a violin again after a year's forced study. He was, however, happy to be of service to them, and in his own affable and indulgent way, to her. She sighed quixotically as she hurried from rehearsal, clutching her violin case as if it were a lance.

Johnnie – her brother – had always insisted on holding their rendezvous at the loathsome Russian Tea Room,
maybe because he could remind her that she still hadn't
played Carnegie Hall, the creep. This time, when he made
his entrance – late, as usual – her heart leapt into her throat
despite herself.

Unshaven, pale and sweaty notwithstanding the season,
he moved towards her slowly with the stiff laborious gait
of an elderly invalid. His eyes roved incessantly, alighting at
random on various points like a nervous fly, and his lips had
lost their fixed smirk. In his salad days he had had the smug
good looks of an oblivious athlete, and his looks had carried
him through the challenges of an itinerant lifestyle into middle age. But now she saw a spectre, and she wilted.

'Hey sis, it's been a while,' he muttered, depositing a large
stuffed shopping bag under their table. He bent his tobacco-
scented head towards hers and she lightly pressed her cheek
against his, caught between wanting to embrace him wildly,
despite her aversion to cigarettes, and wanting to flee.

'What's that, crocodile tears?' he sneered, taking his seat.

Fury at this callous but typical remark, informed by the
long and familiar litany of troubles and disgrace, steeled her
and she reverted to form. 'What a fool!' she accused herself
– and him – making ready to depart.

'Sit down,' Johnnie commanded, 'I don't want any of your
money. Let's order something, it's on me.'

'On *you*? You look – Johnnie, what's wrong?'

'Waiter, give her anything she wants,' he called out cava-
lierly. 'You want a vodka? I'll take a vodka, straight up, just
like the Russians,' he chuckled ghoulishly.

It took several vodkas for her to relax into a passable civil-
ity. They hardly spoke, Johnnie making a show of ogling

every attractive woman either seated or entering the joint, all pitifully hollow bravado. She studied his face, noting the pockmarks and slightly skewed teeth that made him still seem menacing. Who was he? What had happened to him? How could he turn out like this? The same unanswerable questions, now given poignancy by his obvious physical decrepitude and the heavy foreboding of unasked-for responsibility.

'Johnnie, what do you want? Are you ... ' The accusation hung like a thick and putrid dew.

'I'm taking care of myself, just like you. Don't worry, it's age.' He coughed. 'But you're looking good – I saw the review last month, the one that mentioned your arms.'

Julia blushed, recalling her colleagues' response to the critic whose grasp of music paled in comparison to his prurience. But as they said, any publicity was good publicity. Maybe.

'Where are you living now?'

'Queens.'

'Where exactly in Queens?' she retorted impatiently.

'Wherever I want – what are you, a cop?'

Johnnie was now perspiring copiously. What began as a laugh quickly became an unstoppable cough, and his rattling wheezes were like blows to her own chest. The cheery, gluttonous and noisy guests took no notice. Still hacking, he rose for the men's room.

When he returned Julia silently took his hand into her own and held it tight, the first time in decades. Her eyes welled up as she told him she loved him, that he was still her brother, no matter what. She fled to the ladies' before he could cut her again.

In that unlikely sanctum she broke down, heaving and sobbing as she squatted on the toilet, giving vent to the miserable guilt and anger and helpless love she felt for this strange miscreant who had squandered his intelligence, his prospects, his degrees, his family and his friends, and who made her feel eternally miserable for succeeding. She recalled the look he had given her when, with their dead alcoholic father in his arms, he had said curtly, 'You're a little too late.'

What damned nerve! It was *he*, Johnnie, with his damned pretentious 'ie' who had driven their father crazy, had preyed upon him, had robbed, defrauded and exploited him, had forced himself into his cramped apartment whenever his luck was down. *She* was the one her father called at midnight threatening to kill the bastard, to cut him off, to do who knows what to her brother, and though she argued and advised, her father always went back for more, concluding with exasperating resignation after each and every rant, 'He's still my son.'

She rose and dabbed her face at the washstand, appraising her reflection. Was it her fault she was pretty and talented, that she had made it out, that she had done something with herself? And in fact she was extremely pretty, in an angular sort of way, like her playing – accurate, precise, driven, with a fast and narrow vibrato (like Toscha Seidel's, she comforted herself, but in truth without its incandescent variety and lyricism).

And now what was she to do?

Fearing he'd bolt, she hurried back to the table. His restlessness and elusive vacancy numbed her.

'I want to help you, Johnnie,' she persisted.

'Yeah, thanks, I don't need any help,' he rasped. 'The party's over, sis.'

'Don't say that!' she shouted, recalling their father's phrase, and quickly cringing as the wait staff turned in her direction.

She fumbled with her purse, hectically extracting several bills and pressing them into his hands.

'Take it and shut up. Now, give me your doctor's number.'

Johnnie absently complied.

'When am I going to see you again?' she demanded.

'Soon. I'll be in touch, sis.'

'Will you? I have to leave the country for a while, but I'll be back next month.'

Johnnie shrugged. 'Yeah, like always.'

'Stop it,' she hissed, 'I'm trying to help. It's not like you deserve it.'

Johnnie rose at the insult with a grimace, grabbed his bag and shuffled his way to the door, nodding contemptuously over his shoulder.

'Get back here!' she cried, upsetting a glass of water.

By this time he was out and into the grey winter's night, one among the many.

* * *

Julia walked briskly to her hotel room. Juan, the luthier, was waiting.

'Well?' he inquired eagerly.

'That son of a bitch,' Julia smiled. Sure enough, the fiddle she removed from her case was not the one she had brought with her. It was in fact a cheap beginner's model, made of course in China.

'As I see it,' she confided to Juan between the sheets, 'it's a win-win. He gets to pawn what he thinks is my Guadagnini, thanks to you, darling.' She gave her lover a grateful peck for the convincing replica he had crafted. 'That will buy me at least three years of freedom. Oh, and I called his "doctor" on my way here – she's apparently an expert in massage.'

As Juan slept the sleep of the contented, Julia stole stealthily out of bed and gazed out at the not so starry night sky. A heavy weary sadness pressed into her, as if from the city itself, and she quickly and noiselessly dressed.

Outside Penn Station, with hours to kill before the Boston train, she took out her fiddle. There despite the cold she played for the drunks and drifters, hustlers and vagrants, for the reptilian cabbies and their cargo, for the ceaseless stream of youth, rich and poor, that went their uncomprehending midnight ways, and, finally, for herself.

Violin Caprice No. 8

She heard his breathing from her bedroom and thought the breaths should be more like long, slow and very soft bow strokes stretching out infinitely in time and diminishing in volume to the faintest pianissimo. Instead they were like the spiccato bowing she'd been practicing on the open strings. And then what? What happened to the sounds she made on her violin after they were played? What would happen to her grandfather?

The head she saw in the casket at his viewing shocked her with its bulbous nose, unnaturally ruddy cheeks and thick jet-black hair: he looked like a comic-book Dracula. Well, okay, her grandfather *did* have a big nose, but he never wore make-up and his real hair was like the hair of her bow, a sort of yellowish-white. Who had done this to him? She recoiled fearing that the memory of his kisses would be poisoned, ran to her mother's arms and, finally, cried her heart out. All of her relatives looked on with appreciative sentimental affection, for they assumed she was dutifully grieving in her child's way, when really, she was crying more out of anger and outrage at the undertaker's desecration. The rosary that was intertwined in the chalky fingers of the carcass convinced her it was an impostor's, for her grandfather never prayed, unless wishing for someone to be visited by the IRS were considered prayer, whatever the IRS was, which she assumed to be something pretty frightening.

Later that night she asked her father, whose grief had been worn away in advance by the past six months of illness and caretaking and now showed merely in a frown, where her grandfather went. Being an inveterate atheist, he just couldn't bring himself to speak in fairy tales about heaven, so he compromised, with what he assumed to be paternal assurance: Granddad was still around and still alive in the feelings and memories of those who knew him and loved him.

'And what about the ones who didn't like him?' she queried, 'Is he alive for them too?'

'Well, er, yeah, I guess so,' he added uncomfortably, remembering quite a few people whom his father had pissed off in his time, including himself.

'So what you're saying is that it's like when I play my violin.'

'Uh ... '

'Come on, Dad, when I play a note, where does it go?'

'Into our ears?' he replied cautiously, for his daughter, not unlike his father, was quick in temper.

'Not just into our ears, but everywhere. Look, wait.' She ran and fetched her fiddle. 'Now, when the hairs of my bow rub the string, like so' – and she demonstrated with a "B" on the A string – 'it makes vibrations that vibrate the bridge, that then vibrates the wood on the violin, especially the top, just like you told me, and that shakes the air inside it and around it, and the air particles all have energy which in our human ears we hear as sound. And like we learned at school energy can't be destroyed, *ever*,' she added emphatically, 'it just gets *changed*. So it's somewhere, whether we recognise it or not. So granddad is ... '

'Here, there and everywhere,' her father chimed in.

'Exactly! And even though he can't buy me ice cream and pizza like before, you and mom can, so in a way he can still do regular things, sort of.'

'Honey,' called her father to his wife, 'come here and listen to your daughter, hurry up.'

She repeated her discourse to her mom, adding, '*Our* ears only hear a bit of the energies because Junior can hear things we can't (Junior being their dog). So there are all kinds of invisible energies that must change the universes.'

'The universes?' asked her mother.

'You don't think there's just one, do you, mom?'

The precocious nine-year-old frowned, before declaring aloud like a lawyer to a jury, 'I think music is a special energy that the best parts of us get squeezed into.'

When it was time for bed she hugged her parents much more tightly than usual and whispered to her father, 'That Beatles song is pretty cheesy, Dad.'

And so the energies of Jennifer's life changed. She could see and hear her grandfather in her head, but it was hard to live inside there all the time and he was not so vivid as he was before, and not at all tangible. She missed his pinching her cheeks and stroking her long fine hair. Practicing the violin wasn't nearly as much fun anymore because he loved and applauded everything she did, no matter how it sounded, whereas her father was much more particular and occasionally grew frustrated and even angry. It got to the point where Jennifer's teacher had to speak privately to her dad. For a while he was less demanding: but only a while. After her supervised nightly practice sessions she retreated to her bedroom, propped up the fiddle on a pillow as if it were a teddy bear, and confided her woes, often falling asleep as she did.

One day after school she had come home to find Junior happily gnawing away at the neck of her violin and drooling all over her bed. She screamed at the Irish Setter and yanked his ear and smacked him on the snout. It was the first time she had ever struck the animal and she burst into tears as Junior scampered away, shutting her door lest anyone discover what had occurred. What would her father say?

A string was broken, which was no big deal, and there were a number of teeth marks near the nut. Her dad would be furious and she would be punished not so much by restrictions, because she didn't do anything besides go to school, practice and play soccer on weekends, and anyway it would be a reward not to have to play soccer, but by her father's irascibility, which had grown steadily worse. Yes, she realised, he was very highly strung.

So one by one she jerked and broke each of the remaining strings. She then carefully laid the violin on the floor and gingerly stood on its belly as if testing the strength of ice on a pond. It resisted her weight at first, but gradually gave way as she bounced, cracking and sagging unevenly, though still intact. She stepped away, leapt into the air and landed on the instrument with both feet, half a dozen times, before it eventually flattened and splintered. Stricken however with a stomach-sickening dread almost immediately after such frenzied pleasure, she hastened to gather the remaining fragments into an old blanket and stuffed the bundle into the recesses of her closet. She unlocked and lifted her window as high as it would go, positioning her violin case upside down nearby.

Her parents bought it and Jennifer's father had already begun compiling a list of likely neighbourhood suspects, the first of whom lived next door, a nasty little single-parent punk who had several times invited the attention of the local cops for lighting leaf-fires in the gutters. The boy's cowed mother yelled and screamed at her son, whom she knew was no angel, and then ransacked his room but couldn't find a thing. Jennifer's father, thinking the brat had secreted it outside the home, kept pressing the issue the entire week until the thief's mother threatened to sue him for harassment, at which point the sleuthing ceased. Every time he saw the kid he smiled a little smile that said, 'You'll get yours someday.'

The next weekend Jennifer had a "new" 1920s German violin, a step up from her previous model, and things seemed to be better for quite some time: she loved its rich overtones and easy action and her dad had become much more lenient and protective towards her, now that he understood the depth of the envy she excited by her exceptional abilities.

The acquisition of the new instrument coincided with her introduction to vibrato, which Jennifer grasped and produced almost immediately, to her teacher's astonishment. She began to experiment, endlessly, with various ways to create it, using mainly her wrist or her knuckles as focal points, or even the higher joints on her fingers, and making a pitch oscillate in all kinds of ways. She thought of vibrato principally as a means of imparting a special kind of energy to a sound. She was obsessed with vibrato, fascinated by it, delighted with its possibilities and convinced that it connected her with her grandfather in space-time across the universe(s). It was as if she were making technicolour movies from faded old black and white family photographs. She discovered for herself how the smallest, most minute change of pressure or movement from her fingertips produced a change of tone: she almost began to believe in heavens when the instrument opened up. Soon she was eliciting serious praise from the music department at her Academy. The word "prodigy" was being whispered – which was quite over the top but which nevertheless sent her father into ecstasy – and action.

It was clear to him that Jennifer had already outgrown her string teacher, so it was time to make a change, not for the better, but for the best. Professor X, whose students included the famous W, Y and Z, was adamant in no longer taking new pupils, but under the appropriate conditions, one of which would of course include a hefty donation to the conservatory with which he was affiliated, he might relent.

Jennifer's father refinanced their home, albeit against his wife's wishes, and at anxious length secured a promise from the impossible pedagogue (rumoured to like his Scotch, but that's beside the point) to hear her, nothing more. Given this single chance, itself a tremendous victory, her dad made a bold executive decision to maximise the odds of his daughter's acceptance: he was, after all, an executive, wasn't he? Why risk having Jennifer play in the stuffed confines of a studio, where she would be prey to nerves, when she could shine at an actual performance? As the Academy was a prestigious one whose Board was a Who's Who of city potentates, the aged Professor agreed to attend the latter half of Jennifer's school recital, at which she, the only Lower School student, would be featured, six months hence. A chauffeur and limousine naturally went without saying.

Fate, however, has its own designs.

A tall, thin and very pimply-faced boy four years Jennifer's senior attended the advanced music classes with her. She took little notice of him until one day, when he sat at the piano, his pimples completely disappeared.

To play the Brahms *Intermezzi* at the age of thirteen as if he were an ancient soul ... he saddened and bewitched her with these transporting miniatures. For his part he seemed terribly interested in her ardour for vibrato, often lamenting the piano's woeful invariability when it came to pitch. Like her he had a pass from sport, and spent time after school in the music rooms where, under the watchful eye of a tutor, they began to collaborate on Brahms' *Sonata No. 3*. It was initially hard going but such a relief from unaccompanied Bach, which her father now relentlessly and exclusively demanded she focus on in preparation for the Big Event. She thought the shock of dark hair that hung over the boy's right eye was very cute.

The joys of dependent musical anticipation, timing and phrasing delighted her, so used to playing alone. It was like kissing without touching lips. When Gibraltar (what were his parents thinking?) introduced her, with their tutor's permission, to a recording of Joe Venuti and Eddie Lang, she cried because her grandfather had played the same record many times and she had almost forgotten it. He took the guitar part on piano and she imitated Venuti's riffs. She rushed home, throwing herself breathlessly into her father's arms with the news.

'Let's get back to Bach,' he responded drily.

Her mother, who was about as musical as a frog, offered sympathy but no real support.

The worst was to come. As the days to the recital dwindled, it was the Bach *B minor Partita*, over and over, endlessly, and every time she attempted to spice it up with her imaginative variations of vibrato, sometimes fast and wide, sometimes slow and narrow, and everything in between as the moods of the music and her whims seemed to dictate, her dad grew furious.

'Bach was pure!' he shouted. 'The Professor will NOT be impressed!'

She objected by informing him, correctly, that Bach himself didn't really indicate how it should be played except for the notes, and her father who was quite prepared to accept her genius as an instrumentalist, rejected these forays into musicology.

'You may be the Boy Mozart, but you're not his father,' he cryptically admonished.

Whatever. The more her father insisted, the wilder and more colourful her vibrato became, and the more adventurous and unorthodox became her Bach. Out of his earshot. What would her grandfather think?

On the nerve-wracking afternoon of the performance her father was scarcely containable. Jennifer's mother, who had made an art-form of calming her spouse, had reached her limit. The poor man, insisting on a real rather than pre-fabricated bow-tie, couldn't even manage the knot so she eventually did the honours.

During the first half of forgettable mush, he fretted that the Professor would renege. To his blissful relief at intermission, he spied the limo and rushed to greet His Eminence, nearly shaking the hand off him and hovering about like an unwanted moth all the way to the Professor's chair at centre-stage. He seated himself along with his wife in the second row, behind and just to the side of the great man, the better to gauge his reactions.

Jennifer emerged onstage, gay and confident, and she looked stunning, STUNNING, he thought, though the gangly kid cut a sorry figure, what with his pimples and worn velour jacket. They opened with an excerpt, the third movement of the Brahms, and Gibraltar was good enough to allow his daughter to shine, yes, a decent accompanist, no more, but that's all he had to be.

The Professor appeared unmoved, but obviously alert. Although the audience erupted in applause he kept his hands apart. Jesus Christ, couldn't he hear? No, that was his wont, her father recalled: he promised to *listen*, no more, that was all. He must be savouring the morsel.

The duo reappeared and his little girl – and wasn't she quite mature-looking with that hair-do and those sparkly things flecked on her cheeks – approached the front of the stage to announce an unprogrammed "surprise."

Surprise, what surprise? We didn't need surprises, did we? Was she nuts? Gibraltar shyly took his post at the piano and goddamit they played his goddamned father's music, and everyone knew the Professor was NOT interested in jazz!

'Honey,' cooed his wife, 'please relax, sit down and enjoy it.' She was grateful that the Professor turned ever so slightly in his direction so that she could gently press him back into the seat he threatened to vacate in agitation, taking his hand by way of precaution.

It was over within minutes and the audience, who had been swaying and smiling, applauded, hooting, hollering and whistling for more. The Professor blew his nose.

'It's going to be alright,' whispered Jennifer's mom encouragingly.

Jennifer soon re-emerged, now thankfully and gloriously alone, to present the evening's crowning gem, the Bach. As she deftly retuned her instrument the Professor cleared his throat and checked his watch.

Jennifer's father shrank. 'Did you see that?' he said to his wife, 'did you see that?'

'What?'

'Sssshhhh!' admonished the couple next to them.

She confidently began the First Partita – with vibrato. Not occasional, ornamental vibrato, but vibrato on every single note, inescapable, ceaseless, ever-changing vibrato, to her father's unfathomable horror. What the hell did she think she was doing? Bach wasn't meant to be played like that! He made it halfway through the Allemande before leaning forward and advising the Professor: 'She's better than this, believe me!' He tried surreptitiously to signal to his daughter but Jennifer, ever more immersed in the music, was oblivious as a dervish. His gestures grew increasingly large and frantic, disturbing those around him and warranting a stern glance from the Academy's Principal that went unheeded. Atheist though he was, a Higher Power must have taken control, for the frenzied father rushed the stage as if possessed, and as he lunged for his screaming daughter's violin Gibraltar appeared from nowhere to bring him down by the ankles. During the ensuing melee, the Professor slid away unnoticed.

The very next day Jennifer's mother received a hand-delivered letter with deckled edges. He, the Professor, would be privileged to take her daughter into his studio, on the following conditions: firstly, that his services would be rendered gratis and, secondly and most importantly, that her father have absolutely positively utterly definitively and thoroughly nothing, and he meant nothing, whatsoever to do with her musical training.

Several months later on the anniversary of her grandfather's death Jennifer and her parents visited the cemetery. Instead of flowers they brought the shattered remains of a fiddle to scatter on his grave. She thought he approved, wherever he was.

Violin Caprice No. 9

Despite being a violinist David Jones, just recently if some-what dubiously dubbed as an emerging Goliath of his instru-ment, kept up on current events, principally through the online editions of the New York Times, the Washington Post, the International Herald Tribune, CNN, MSNBC and a smattering of left-leaning websites for ballast. During the buildup to the Wars, he noted astutely that the reporting and political analysis of foreign policy appeared virtually identi-cal with the Pentagon's assessment, time and time again. It so happened that just as he smarted from a preposterously ignorant review of a Philadelphia recital, a recital at which he had played his heart out and was, in terms of technique, unas-sailable, another humanitarian invasion was underway and the press reaction was predictably in keeping with the official storyline, so much so that the similarity of language between the government and the Fourth Estate gave him an idea.

'Sol,' he confided to his agent, 'let me ask you a question. You remember what Carl Flesch said about music critics, that one out of a hundred actually knows something about the violin?'

'If that,' replied the elfin Sol.

'And the newspapers and websites are cutting back on their coverage of classical music, am I right?'

'Not to mention their coverage of everything else.'

'Here's what I have in mind.'

And so before his next engagement, an all-Beethoven programme in Pittsburgh a month later, David hosted a dinner
for the local press and selected musical luminaries at one of
the city's fanciest restaurants. Sol made sure that each reviewer
received what amounted to a dossier on Beethoven's life, its
relation to the compositions of the works being played, and
– and here was the delicate part – David's aspirations in performance. For example, "Mr. Jones, in the slow movement
of the sonata, *will attempt* to convey the magisterial melancholy of the theme using a tone with lushness and depth but
without sentimentality ... " and "With scintillating staccato
bowing Mr. Jones will endeavour to reveal the fiery mystery
of the master's reflections upon the tragedy of mortal life
on the verge of extinction...." Etc. It was, admittedly, risky,
but the morning after proved an unmitigated success: they
ate it up. The reviews were unanimous in praise of his interpretation and ability, the phrases he had suggested finding
their way into print nearly without alteration. To their unexpected delight the reviewers themselves were commended by
their editors for an uncommon show of erudition.

Thus David took America by storm and after a few years
had attained most of what he wished. He and Sol tinkered
with their materials, sometimes planting several critical
comments for the sake of verisimilitude, comments such as
"Whereas one might quibble with Mr. Jones' selection of
tempi, in particular his execution of an andante passage at a
brisker pace than usually assayed, the effect he is seeking to
create by contrast allows him to expose the searing vacilla-
tions ... " and so forth. Not only had David helped himself,

but he helped simultaneously to raise the collective intelligence of North American music criticism.

On the Continent, his reputation already secure, the
method worked just as spectacularly. Any qualms about
the greater expertise of European critics were allayed by
their love of indolence: he had made it easy for everybody.
In truth David was that rare musician with popular appeal
and extremely fine and uncompromising musical taste. His
personality was a jovial and generous one and though not
blessed with patrician good looks – in fact he was rather
short and pudgy, with coarse features to boot – it was impossible to resist his open-natured charm and impossible not to
forgive his peccadilloes. Frequently his former wives and lovers sat together in harmony at his concerts.

There was, however, a thorn in his side. When one
describes the German as a failed bassoonist, one has said
everything, but it became a point of honour for David to
win over this stickler, this determined quibbler who not only
had the chutzpah to refuse his concert materials, but insisted
on damning his every Berlin performance with an especially
malevolent faintness of praise. "Herr Jones for pure dexterity has probably surpassed Paganini, and thus rendered the
Ninth Caprice with great feeling and exhilaration; however,
subtle facets of tone were not as prominently in evidence as
one might have desired, though on the whole he satisfied the
audience with sensational playing."

The gall of that man! In the past he had also quibbled over
the so-called liberties David took with the static score, for
example, interpolated notes, changes in phrasing, irregular tempi, stylistically divergent cadenzas, rubato, absence
of rubato, slides, lack of slides, rate of vibrato, and so on
– in short, everything that made music alive. The height

of impertinence came when he referred to David's earth-
ily haunting rendition (so his honest ex-wives told him) of
Debussy's *Beau Soir* as "woollen long-johns music," which
in German came out as one interminable and unpronounce-
able word.

At the Berlin soiree on the night before David's land-
mark performance of the Brahms Concerto à la Joachim,
who debuted the great piece under the composer's aegis, the
bassoonist could be seen sipping a glass of lemon water and
asking whether the hors d'oeuvres were gluten-free, all after
disdaining the succulent and lavishly expensive pâté and
caviar on the grounds of veganism, which David believed
to be a punishable offence in Germany, or close to it. David
approached and, delicate sausage in hand, informed him that
the modern world would hear on the morrow the Brahms
as Brahms himself had heard it – not with the imposition
of sloppy and false Romantic ideals exemplified by the cloying oscillation of pitch on sustained notes which he, David,
would never deign to call a true vibrato, but by the subtle
excitement and tension imparted by a virility of bowing and
a nimbly vivacious use of the left hand. In short, the most
Brahmsian of Brahms, as Joachim introduced it to the world,
though now with perhaps a more varied and robust tonal
palette.

The reviews that poured in, abetted by David's support-
ing documentation, were ecstatic, with one exception, an
exception who wrote: "Surely the maestro's performance was
played in the authentic style of our dear giant, but it may not
have been what Brahms in his innermost ear imagined."

Brahms' innermost ear! It took several weeks for David's
fury to abate. He had been irked of course by the bassoonist's
quip, which in itself had only the bite of a gnat. The residual

itch however had graver implications, for David admitted at length to a greater anger connected with a terrifying truth: his chafing at the demands of the written score. More and more over the years his reverence for composers diminished and had recently, so he honestly confessed, utterly disappeared. Their great, glorious, wondrous works ... what did they themselves really know of them? What were their inanimate and merely approximate symbols without the skills of a performer to infuse life and breath? Never in thousands of years could a composer, no matter how persnickety, stubborn, grandiose and meticulous, direct the multitudinous textures, shades and nuances, the impulsion and shaping that he, the violinist, rendered audible! David had tired of subservience and decided to throw off the reins.

* * *

Before his next Berlin recital, after the mysterious absence of a year from the concert stage, he surprised his guests by announcing the discovery, on a pilgrimage to the home of his ancestors in Spain, of a cache of manuscript scores from his great-great-great grandfather, a Marrano from Barcelona who had migrated to Campo de Criptana where he secretly devoted his life to the composition of music honouring his faith and the culture of the Sephardim. David apologised for the dearth of the usual voluminous information he supplied, as he was busying himself in the transcription of a musical language that for him, he modestly averred, had no precedent.

The bassoonist coughed up a rice cracker and his colleagues grew anxious, for they would now have to do a bit of unaccustomed but actual journalistic work. The food and drink were, nevertheless, as superb as ever, which was a comfort.

The curious recital, at which David presented a series of miniatures, self-invented pastiches of Sarasate, Achron, Corelli, Ysaÿe, Farina and Enescu, graced by his own practiced ornaments, enchanted the audience, although his encore left them baffled and bemused.

Next morning the quiescently ecstatic David was delighted to read in the Anarchist broadsheet for which the bassoonist wrote not only that he had transcended the instrument and discovered for himself a new career, but that with his culminating *Partita for Violin without Strings* he had liberated both performer and listener from the confines of the audible, thus heralding boundless imaginative possibilities.

And so, David chuckled, he supposed he had!

Violin Caprice No. 10

My dad, the surgeon, and not just any kind of surgeon but a cardio-thoracic one, liked to challenge me, which was fine. Like the time we were skiing Lake Louise and he said, 'Do the men's downhill without killing yourself and you've got yourself a new pair of skis.' Motivation. Somehow I managed to scrape and slide my way down what was a pure sheet of ice at about 100 miles an hour and dad kept his word. Nice skis too.

But it was the challenges I *didn't* know were challenges that irked me, which he was pulling all the time. Example: biking up a hill together, a steep and endless one, he looked over at me just as we heaved our way to the summit and punched the tab on his wristwatch. 'You missed an upgrade by two seconds, son.' By upgrade he meant a new bike, which I was very keen on. That was dad, a garden-variety C-T surgeon.

Naturally he expected me to follow in *his* footsteps, certainly not mom's: she was a pathologist, a respected one, but, well, the personalities differed, lucky for me. He loved her but he cracked that "bedside manner" joke a few too many times, and as I got into my teens it began to sound a bit creepy. Then it was 'At least she's not a flea,' by which he meant not a GP or internist, you know, *the last thing to leave a dying patient*. Which I thought was more genuinely funny. You might say that, professionally speaking, they had anatomy in common, ha ha. Come to think of it I'm creeping myself out. Long story short, it was anatomy that sold dad on my taking a year off before starting med school. Mom was cool with it but he needed encouragement to bestow his blessing on my delaying the unstoppable juggernaut of my burgeoning career by a whole year.

Let me explain. I'd worked my butt off in college doing pre-med and almost nothing else, and in my senior year, after I had already been accepted at Penn, I stacked up advanced physiology, genetics and neuroanatomy *when the grades didn't even count*. I needed a break before what I knew would be at least eleven straight years full bore to get to the promised land: four at med school, five residency and two fellowship, at least. Maybe more. I was up for it, but I just needed a break, I needed to do something I'd never have the chance to do again easily. Italy, Italian art, and Italian girls, mountains, coasts, incredible food, archaeology, a little wine (I'm not much of a drinker), but mainly Florence – Firenze! – Florentine art, architecture and girls, in ascending order of priority. I'd been to two week-long conferences there with my parents when I was in high school and it just blew me away, wandering around the streets of the Medici, museums and churches and art everywhere, everywhere. I almost had my first real kiss there.

The art bit came mainly from my mom. Her path slides looked like abstract art anyway, and she was forever sketching out histological specimens. But back to my story. What clinched it for dad was when I showed him that I'd already arranged for a brief but official internship at La Specola, a museum near the Pitti Palace famous for wax anatomical sculptures used to teach medicine and for killing the trade in cadavers (I've got my dad's sense of humour). He gave me his OK, grudgingly, but nothing else: not even a dime, the skinflint. Another one of his challenges. Mom at least sprang for airfare. I'd saved enough dough from MCAT tutoring (I took the MCATs early and nailed them) to get me through six months if I was careful. So I decided to bring my violin, which I personally thought was a stroke of genius.

Why a violin? First, it's small and easily portable. Second, it's not a guitar. Everybody plays guitar in Europe. There's a busker at every damned park or streetcorner. Not a lot of violins. In fact, I couldn't remember a single one when we were there. Third, appeal, meaning a fiddler is going to attract not your everyday punk-rock fanatic or droopy hippy chick, but someone with a little more going on above the eyebrows. Not that I'm a snob, because I wasn't about to play the Bach Partitas: I couldn't, I can't, and I never will. I mean my repertoire is basically hillbilly, Irish, a dozen or so French salon pieces (my mom's French) and any local folk or pop tune I can pick up by ear, which for me is pretty easy.

It's not like I had a lot of time for the violin in college aside from doing the party thing. I knew way before that serious classical wasn't for me. Did you ever see a classical violin student smile or look like they're having fun? Of course not, they're like tortured souls from the *Inferno*: nothing they do is ever good enough, they're always worrying about intonation, and when their intonation is okay they fret about their sound, is it big or *beautiful* enough, etc. They act like the piano is an inferior instrument. And they also say things like, 'If I had so-and-so's technique with my musicality ... ' Not appealing.

Well, I flew into Zurich (cheapest fare) and took the train through the Alps all the way to Florence. Going through the mountains was like a dream, something out of a James Bond movie, and I marvelled that this could be happening to me, just like that. When we broke clear and hit the plains I was beaming and I wasn't shy about practicing my Italian on anyone who came into my carriage. The dream-like scenario continued when at long last I arrived in Florence at night smack in the middle of the Feast of San Giovanni. It was like being on the set of a Fellini film! Jet-lagged beyond description but too excited to care, I drank in the crowds and festivities as I wandered my way to a pensione close to Santa Maria Novella. The unreality of that reality cut my tether to the past four years, instantaneously, and I was ready for adventure.

It took a few weeks to get into a routine and for me to figure out that absolutely nothing was open from about noon to four. It being summer, the mosquitoes were like marauding Huns and because medieval Florentine dwellingplaces couldn't have screens I had to burn a putrid insecticide all night long on a hot plate at my bedside. A lot of folks are down on the States, but the American window screen is nothing to be scorned, not to mention air conditioning. Plus I had to get over the nauseating stench of Vespa fumes that invaded the city centre each morning and hung in the air like an immoveable suffocating blanket. I shifted around looking for better digs but in my price range they were all pretty much the same: hot, noisy, full of tourists, with hygienically-challenged dormitory bathrooms. One of them served coffee that was made the night before in a large vat, which I discovered when I sneaked into the kitchen. In Italy. Hard to believe.

I eventually made my way to the Oltr'Arno, the working class neighbourhood across the river where rents and meals were a lot cheaper and where I looked forward to the luxury of my own private "doccia" or shower. It was private all right, but to call the pencil thin dribble of water an actual shower was like calling the Torc waterfall in Killarney Niagara Falls. Fortunately it was just out of reach of the hordes of tourists and served as a good base for my explorations. Now that I was settled I could develop a bit of a rhythm: rise early, throw up (the Vespas), quick breakfast, meander, stop at any church that took my fancy, any building, any museum, head back to my side of town for a workingman's meal, my main one of the day, and then a siesta because there was nothing else to do. Up again, more wandering, a few groceries to bring back to the flat and then bed or a bit of nightlife.

You may not believe this but the most striking thing I experienced during those first three months was shoes. Women's shoes. Women's shoes on display in virtually every street, in shoe-stores filled with a variety that rivalled the number of insect species. Every conceivable (for me, inconceivable) shape, type, colour, size, style, made from every imaginable material, though I must say they tended to be more on the high spindly heeled or ornate sandal side. I was mesmerised and often I would spend half an hour before a shop window taking it all in while slyly watching the clientele who packed the places and spent thousands upon thousands of lire on these, well, fascinating creations.

I was also surprised at how easy it was to spend money: my six-month allowance had nearly disappeared, so I was forced to bring out the fiddle. Let me tell you something: even though my father was a surgeon and I was going to be a surgeon, there are some things that can dent my confidence. Playing country fiddle in summertime in Florence was one of them, but I bit the stiff upper lip. It was either that or calling home and hearing the old man smirk over the phone. I hauled out the violin a few blocks from the Ponte Vecchio where three shoe-stores converged, usually late afternoons and early evenings. I made just enough to keep going, but the side benefits I had expected never materialised: for every good looking tourist chick there were at least a dozen extremely well-tailored and painfully handsome Italian men hovering around. An American in baggy jeans didn't stand a chance, with or without a violin. I was truly bummed. As for the Italian women, well, if any of them ever looked at me I'd never have known it, because they kept their eyeballs focussed like laser beams on whatever was either nonhuman or feminine, my theory being that it was a way to survive the predatory opposite sex of their native land. Incidentally, I ended up making most of my money playing the theme from *The Godfather*. Okay, I'm ashamed, but I had little choice.

This put me well and truly in the dumps and I did something out of character. After another hot and lonely busking session I hauled out a bottle of Chianti, one with the black rooster on the label, and trundled home slowly, pausing to lift its contents to my lips every few blocks until I had downed the whole damn thing. I felt better – in fact, I felt mighty fine – until on the street approaching my pensione I stumbled over several inconveniently placed cobblestones and gashed my head. A little throbbing, not a big deal, except I couldn't quite get to my feet. Next thing the landlady was screaming and had fetched her husband. They were nice people but they didn't understand that the scalp, being highly vascular, bled out from a mere scratch, and I tried to tell them so, in somewhat imperfect Italian as I lay on the ground, and that I was going to be a surgeon and that everything would be okay, even if my right hand was copiously drenched in blood from touching my wound.

People were gathering around me, the feet of many, and as I turned my woozy head I saw an incredibly stunning pair of elegant shoes the colour of a vintage Stradivarius, a kind of burnished copper. We all know a shoe is only as good as the foot it holds, and before I blacked out I thought that those delicately crafted specimens had to be the most absolutely wonderful in the world. I could have kissed them.

When I awoke in my room at the pensione the landlady was keeping a bedside vigil with a rosary, rising every once in a while to peer anxiously into my face and shaking me virtually every time I began to doze. The next day I got a glimpse of the damage I had done: a huge shiner and a gash that must have required at least ten stitches. They insisted on bringing me to the doctor who had serendipitously come to my rescue and whose offices were nearby.

A rather tall beautiful woman with a smirk just like my old man's greeted me. I told her I was there to see the doctor.

'I am the doctor.'

With that figure – and those shoes? So this is who buys them? When she carefully palpated my wound it wasn't pain that I felt. She had me walk a bit, checked my gait, tested my strength bilaterally, and used the ophthalmoscope, a typical gross neuro exam. Except that when she examined my optic nerves her lustrous subtly scented hair fell to one side and brushed my cheeks. Talk about tachycardia!

'Come back in seven days and I'll remove the stitches. You'll be okay if you stay away from our lovely Italian wine.'

'Grazie, *Dottore*,' I answered with Continental suavity, or so I imagined, blushing deeply.

It's amazing what a deadline can do. Seven days! I had seven days to prepare myself for Dr. Ricci's touch (even if she wore latex gloves), seven days to ready myself for a look of studied indifference as she bent her beautiful face close to my own to do her work, seven days to figure out something meaningful to say that would prolong our encounter. Hell, we were practically colleagues anyway, so we'd have plenty to talk about, wouldn't we?

First, I needed some threads, which meant I needed some money. I discovered how generous people could be to a pathetic-looking busker: my black and swollen eye which I could barely open, and the cut above its brow roused the giving spirit and in just three days I had taken in more than during the previous three weeks. Hmmmm ... something to mull over in future. Next, I studied the Italian guys, the ones with the cute Germans or Swedes on their arms, for sartorial tips. Finally, I got a haircut – well, not just a cut, but a *styling*. I prayed that the swelling on my head would subside enough for me to look less grotesque – and I also used lots of ice.

On the seventh day I hyperventilated my way into Dr. Ricci's office and as I rose to greet her she impulsively burst into laughter.

'You look like an Italian gigolo!' she exclaimed, before gathering herself and offering apologies.

I was mortified, and speechless.

'Come, Mr. American, let me see what I can do.' The stitches took a few dreamy minutes and as I awkwardly attempted to thank her for helping me, as I tried to screw up my courage to tell her that I was about to go to med school and to ask her about practice, to see whether she had heard of my dad – I caught a glimpse of her shoes, exquisitely ornate and red, which exposed the white instep of her arched olive foot. She caught me looking as if I hadn't looked and pretended that she hadn't noticed my looking or understood that my tachycardic heart was now in my throat.

'I guess it's a good thing I wandered by when you had your accident. Otherwise they would have had the Sisters take you to hospital: to a sick person they look like chaperones to heaven.'

Being unable to speak coherently, I grinned.

'Well, you're all better now.' She had the kind of voice that made a cat's purr sound cacophonous.

I kept grinning, in my seat. She peered at me intently for a moment, beginning to grin a little herself, and then asked, 'Aren't you the boy with the violin near the Ponte Vecchio?'

I bristled at being referred to as a boy, but this broke the ice: she had heard me? It gave me a chance to blurt out everything I could about who I was, why I was there, La Specola, surgery, Dante, art....

'Basta!' she chuckled, stymieing my torrent. 'Have you been to the Bargello?'

'No.'

'You must go. It will be a treat, and is much less crowded than the Uffizi. The "David" of Donatello is there.'

'Thank you, Dottoressa.'

'You may call me Francesca.'

Damn. Nobody ever called my dad by his first name!

'Grazie tante, Dottoressa Francesca.' I'm nothing if not quick.

'Arrivederci, ragazzo.' Touché.

For the next two weeks I plied the fiddle religiously at my usual spot hoping to catch a glimpse of Francesca. I had taken to wearing a patch over my battered eye even after it had healed. Very good for business, though not for surveillance. I scanned the streets in vain. Surely I hadn't misread her, had I? Then on a steamy Thursday evening she appeared on the fringes of my small ragged audience, a parcel in hand,

whose contents were obvious. Her lips were pursed as I seg-
ued quickly from *The Godfather* to Debussy's *Girl with the
Flaxen Hair*. She approached as the Philistines drifted away.

'So let me see your eye,' she said, lifting my patch. 'Are all
Americans as devious as you?'

Before I could think of a clever answer she had suggested
that I accompany her to her flat to keep away the *mosconi*,
Florentine males that pestered attractive women on the
streets like flies. She lived not far from her office, which was
not far from my pensione. As we strolled together I marvelled at the way she negotiated the cobbled streets of the
city with heels of yet another extraordinarily flattering pair
of shoes that seemed so precarious.

'May I buy you a coffee, Francesca?' I queried timidly in
my best Italian manner.

'Why not save your money and allow me to make you a
real coffee? A cup of coffee, nothing more, so don't get any
ideas.'

I had an abundance of ideas, very few of which made it
past my lips as we sat at her modest quarters and simply
talked. I was at first full of philosophy and strong opinion
which she frequently found amusing. She on the other hand
spoke of little things, the way a farmer stroked his chin while
being examined, how she could spot heroin addicts by their
eyes, the shape of coffee-pots, the view from Fiesole, the terrible food in central Florence, and the lovely music in hidden
places all around the city. She spoke of Renaissance art and
I quickly came to understand that I had overestimated my
expertise.

'You cannot see the Uffizi in one day, or one week, or one
month!' she declared. 'And that is only a fraction of what we
have here. Nine months is really not much time.'

She questioned me a little, somehow managing to eke out a love of poetry and an admission that I had tried my hand after attending a James Joyce conference in Dublin during college. Poetry I hadn't shown a soul. And I told her how for me the best part of the Renaissance was a kind of indivisibility between art and science. She might actually have been impressed when I recited a bit from the third canto of the *Inferno*:

> *Caron dimonio, con occhi di bragia*
> *loro accennando, tutte le raccoglie;*
> *batte col remo qualunque s'adagia.*

As I gazed at her, noting the asymmetry of her eyes, the sheen of her light brown hair, the long slender unadorned fingers, the sternocleidomastoid that begged kissing every time she turned her head ... I was just melting. Yes, a far better phrase: "melting in love." It had to be some form of love because when I saw her again the next Thursday I hadn't ceased remembering every utterance and movement of hers. I smiled without cause and couldn't do the simplest thing without wondering what she might think about it. It didn't *feel* dangerous, that I was losing myself in her, but did it even matter who the real her was? We love people not for who they are but for who we half-imagine them to be, the other half kept deliciously unknown. I had another theory about love: if two people liked the way each other looked, sounded and smelled there were definite possibilities, possibilities that touch and taste would definitively resolve.

Of course I learned all kinds of things about her background, her parents (academics in Torino), the unseen poor outside the fascinating centre of Florence whom she was devoted to, her brothers (one an actor, the other a cellist, communists both), and I sensed that something very troubling had happened, involving a man, or men, I don't know, I just picked up something discordant. Why the hell didn't she have a boyfriend? I really didn't want to get into that too deeply because I was flattering myself that with a little luck I just might qualify – until she asked me a very curious favour, and made me an offer any sensible guy would have refused.

She was pregnant, she said, and she wanted her baby to have the benefit of hearing and feeling the rich sounds of a bowed string instrument, a violin, while within her. Would I mind playing my fiddle, those nice French songs or pieces like them, a few evenings a week? She would pay me more than I could earn on the street; and we could continue our talks over coffee afterwards.

Jesus Christ. Crushed. Crestfallen. Demoralised. Damned. Deflated.

But I said yes, except to the money, which I considered an insult (despite my need!). And instead of enriching my soul with the treasures of Florence or any other part of Italy for that matter, I hit the fiddle. No, not literally: I started practicing all day long to build up my repertoire beyond the few salon things I knew, stationing myself far from my previous haunts, but keeping the eye-patch in use. What did I care? The pickings were slim but sufficient. Okay, every once in a while I reverted to that damned theme: I had to!

Francesca generally sat in profile when I played for her at night, hands folded upon her womb. The protrusion was hardly noticeable at first, but it grew inexorably with the passing weeks. She closed her eyes and would occasionally ask me to repeat a song or an air, and complimented me. I played fairly simple but lyrical stuff, omitted any double-stops, and seemed to be creating a decent sound.

Our coffee conversations after the half-hour or so of my performances lasted deeper and deeper into the evening. When two people start talking like that, regularly, and stop worrying about what they say to each other, it's really astonishing what happens – not in words, but in physical sensation and beyond, which I suppose must mean that there *is* something beyond, even if I can't rationalise it. And because I had nothing to lose I could be myself, mostly. One evening as she bade me goodbye at the door I inclined my head and was on the very verge of touching those soft full ruddy lips, when she turned away abruptly. Her peerless eyes told me not to venture there again.

We ventured instead, as her belly grew, to the city. She delighted me with the history of the Signoria and the Piazza della Repubblica, of the competition for the doors of the Baptistry, of the construction of the Duomo and the architecture of the Laurentian Library. She showed me the magnificent frescoes of Masaccio, described Giotto's role in the reawakening of pictorial art, and took me to the church where Dante melted in the presence of his Beatrice. It seemed that in every depicted woman – excepting those of Michelangelo who, let's face it, was more interested in male anatomy than female, and it showed! – I saw her.

I couldn't bring myself to ask about the child, or rather the man responsible for the child, whoever he was, probably some smart rich talented athletic good-looking bastard. I just played, and talked. I'll say this about myself: I never paused to wonder what she saw or didn't see in me – I was too smitten to bother. I did manage, however, to inquire about her shoes. Despite her ever-increasing burden, she continued to

wear the most fashionable, elegant and least practical foot-
wear imaginable. How did she do it?

'Come with me on Saturday and I will give you an answer
to your impertinent question,' she replied in her quaint Ital-
ianate English.

She led me from the Oltr'Arno to Santa Croce, not to the
main church but to the cloister adjacent. There we stood,
just the two of us, before the divine Pazzi Chapel. Passing
slowly through the portico we entered the interior, gazing
up at the sunlit dome, at the lines and light that Brunelleschi
somehow conjured to render a visual harmony that was
extrasensory. Everything about it, the play of circles, arches
and curves, the brilliant glazed della Robbia terracottas, the
fresco of the Florentine night sky, breathed the strength of
balance and beauty.

When one day she told me I hadn't the soul of a true surgeon I took her to La Specola, where my internship was finishing, if you call showing up once a week to say hello to the
Director an internship. As we moved from one faithful wax
model to another of the human body, interior and exterior –
muscles, skin, intestines, liver, the portal circulation, nerves,
arteries, brain, lungs, heart and even the womb with its treas-
ure revealed within – all sculpted and portrayed with cool
uncanny stenchless colourful vivid accuracy, I began to have
doubts. She reached for my hand as we exited and held it on
our return. What could this mean?

As she grew bigger and as my sojourn neared its end I
grew doleful and moody. I found myself fantasising about
her child and on good days convinced myself that the vibrations from my instrument would have an indelibly positive
effect, that I had been transmitting something essential from
a part of me to a part of her, and that he or she might perhaps

become a real musician. On other days, far more frequent, I was convinced she was cruel and crazy, and that I was a helpless fool. I had all but forgotten about my impending medical studies and concentrated on the other impending event. She had become big beyond belief until at last she informed me that she would go to a friend's during the final two weeks before she was expected to deliver. I would still be in Florence when she returned, and I would at least be able to get a glimpse of her child before I resumed a sensible life, though what good that glimpse would do me I could hardly fathom.

Eating little and sleeping hardly at all, I became wretched and at one point tempted to crush the "instrument" of my distress. Some genius I was to bring the damned thing with me.

Then at last when my landlady solemnly delivered a message from the doctor I flew to her flat.

Francesca greeted me with awkward apprehension. She was wearing the Stradivarius shoes, and she looked so beautiful I nearly cried. Her troubled brow made her beauty all the more intense.

'Please sit down, caro,' she said, 'and forgive me! I'm afraid ... I'm afraid ... '

I took a seat on her sofa, bewildered, paralysed. What had happened?

"First, you must promise to forgive me, in advance, and then I can explain."

What could I do but assent in my quietly frenzied way? And forgive her for what? She made coffee, cups and saucers clattering unnaturally. I thought she would break into tears as she sat beside me. She spoke in her native tongue, her rich soft mellifluous voice issuing in heaves and spurts like unfamiliar music in rehearsal, and I understood every word.

'You see, a while ago I met a man, a man I thought was very wonderful, a man I could love and who loved me. I was young and I poured myself into the glorious passion of surrender, but when I slipped he ran away. Yes, I was at fault, I had a fling, quick, impulsive, delightful, but just a fling, nothing at all serious, I swear, but he was too hurt, too sensitive, too unsophisticated maybe ... so he left for Milan. Well, I was young enough to recover from the guilt and loss and I eventually met someone else, just as wonderful but in a different way. This time he was the one who betrayed and I was the one who fled. Maybe I could not love properly? His betrayal was the more lethal because it was a rejection of our love for a greater one, for a woman who eclipsed me in his heart, not a woman to be had or taken lightly. I became a ghost, no, not even a spectre, for a very long time, and I survived only by hurling myself into the greatest of masters, medicine. I am older than you by at least a decade, and I should have known better than to lead you on. If only you hadn't smashed that fine head of yours, or that I hadn't heard you and your violin, those fragments of melody that wrenched me out of a pleasant and calm living! What was I thinking, what am I thinking now? I should never have taken you to the Pazzi Chapel when I knew I was losing myself!'

Caressing my mystified face she wept and then, rising abruptly, led me out of her parlour for the first time and into another room. Pointing to a heap of rags she quietly said, 'There is my child.'

I looked at the bundle of fabric and looked at her, and looked back at the bundle again: stuffing. Stuffing!

'I didn't know whether you would be capable of love, so I had to have proof, over time,' she confessed.

Bit by bit we added our clothes to the mound on the chair and at long last Francesca permitted me delicately and ever so slowly to unfasten the straps of her shoes and toss them too onto the pile.

Firenze, June 1983

Postscript (1992): I stayed in Italy, stayed with medicine too, and eventually joined my darling's practice. Because Francesca refused to allow me to abandon the violin my father took to calling me "The Performing Flea" – initially in scorn but eventually in fondness, the bum.

Violin Caprice No. 11

Call me Bartholomew. It helps. It helps because I'm ugly. Not grotesquely deformed, which would elicit a measure of sympathy, nor plain, which goes unremarked, but ugly, which acts like a kind of centripetal force to push everyone away. Insisting on my full name compels people to engage with me for just that little bit longer, even though it makes them uneasy.

I knew something was terribly amiss by the age of three when my mother, bless her, would say things like 'You're no Clark Gable but I love you.' The photos of my father, whom I never met, showed a dashing roué, a veritable ladies' man. And although my mom, as I eventually discerned when I grew into my teens, was no beauty in the conventional sense, she was far from being ugly. In fact, she was forever warding off suitors, possibly because she had a great deal of charm and wit.

It is very difficult, being ugly, to cultivate charm. In the first place, one must hold an audience long enough for what is charming to be revealed. Which for me was impossible.

The disadvantages of ugly are quite numerous. It is a little known fact that ugly people do not like other ugly people: we are as repulsed as others by ugliness. The strength of our desires for the beautiful is matched only by the depths of our inevitable failure to attain it or to be more precise, her. I supposed that a truly ugly person, if extremely rich, might procure a beautiful girlfriend, or even wife, but even then would be forced to live with the knowledge that avarice overrode aesthetic judgment. A poor consolation.

The Abstract Expressionist painter, Willem de Kooning (who could make beautiful people look ugly), once said the worst thing about being poor was that it took up all of one's time. The same goes for ugly. It is an inescapable ever-present state of being of which one is always aware.

Ugly people tend not to get breaks. For example, a bank employee is unlikely to let an ugly person slip in thirty seconds before closing time for an urgent transaction, whereas a suitably obsequious non-ugly person would have a fifty-fifty chance, and a beautiful one would be guaranteed an extension.

The ugly bleed, cry, grow impatient, lie, steal, become insanely rabid partisans at a football game, hunt for bargains and secretly explore pornography. Our trespasses however are never forgiven because saintliness is demanded of us as the price of social tolerance. We may mingle, if we must, ONLY if we behave.

We sometimes console ourselves with the idea of age, the great leveller that turns even the most beautiful into an ugly, but because the pain of living with ugliness tends to shorten the spans of our lives, even this pleasure is ultimately denied. All in all, ugly is not to be recommended. However, from four decades of experience I conclude that it does confer one distinct advantage: it makes it easy to be alone.

My mother often spoke of inner beauty, of not judging books by covers, of counting what was inside rather than outside, etc., but these concepts were impossible for me to apply to myself because the mirror gave me no outward comeliness to introject. She was determined to mitigate the sorrows of my affliction and in the wisdom arising from desperation she introduced the violin.

'You'll be so good at this that people will love you!' She left out 'despite how you look' but I fully understood.

And indeed I took to the instrument, having long isolated hours at my disposal, and I became very very very good, so good that I was able to obtain employment first with an orchestra and then with several quartets. 'Several quartets?' you may ask. Yes, unusual, and this brings me to the nub.

Music in general and the violin in particular, in addition to providing me with an occupation and one of my few sources of joy, also enabled the discovery that I had perfect pitch, and then some. Not long ago – and I will get to this in a moment – I was retrospectively diagnosed with a very rare disorder: Intolerance of Imperfect Intonation, or the triple "I" syndrome as it is allegedly known in the mental health field.

Whether or not ugly people are more likely to suffer from mental problems requiring professional treatment is unclear. I read often of extremely attractive women and men who require psychiatric and psychological intervention, for problems I would happily absorb if accompanied by such looks, but so be it.

My insistence on perfect pitch from very early on was both blessing and bane. It accounted for my playing with relatively superb intonation, though intonation that was never ideal. This made me a valued ensemble performer while at the same time creating incessant difficulties. For example, I was always painfully cognisant of my failure to achieve the intonation I strove for on the violin, but my colleagues' far more alarming and, sadly enough, routine departures from pitch caused actual physical distress. And because my faculties for discriminating pitch were so finely developed, the vagaries of tuning even for instruments of fixed pitch like the piano, made me wince. Once a joker asked me to tune my fiddle to the A of his tuning fork, which he had had deviously constructed to produce a note vibrating at 443 Hz. I did not find this amusing.

Although I had while quite young been appointed to the first violin section of an orchestra with an international reputation, the maddening divergence from true pitch from all quarters nearly drove me to alcohol. Playing with earplugs insulated me from the worst of it, but the sheer number of off-pitch instruments became overwhelming, inescapable and all-encompassing: in a word, ugly. So I resigned, forfeiting a lucrative lifetime tenure. (I might add that a solo career, which my playing on its own merits might well have sustained, was out of the question owing to my looks.)

I was welcomed into the Andromeda Quartet as the second, and less visible, violin, one of the "inner voices" (as elusive perhaps as inner beauty), and I soon found that the assault of three poorly pitched instruments on my ears was every bit as devastating. I attempted at every opportunity to "lift" the ensemble, which drifted flat often by as much as a quarter-tone, to correct pitch, frequently having to call a halt in the midst of rehearsals, but this seemed to annoy the others to the point of resentment. Whether through inability or sheer laziness, they were impervious to the ideals of playing in proper tune.

The Ciandelli Quartet, whose principal violin had impetuously run off with a software developer on the eve of an important concert featuring the late quartets of Beethoven, beckoned. I hoped that a position of leadership would enable me to exert greater influence. During our last-minute rehearsal of op. 131, which I had memorised, I refused to proceed beyond the first four bars until they were rendered with appropriate – *not* approximate – intonation. When I realised that we would never make it beyond these initial measures I stalked off, glaring at the cellist, who was an especially arrogant and sloppy executant, though not ugly. I learned later that he had virtually pushed the former first violinist, a strikingly curvaceous woman, into the arms of another, having grown weary of her. The concert was cancelled, and rightly so, sparing prospective listeners and Beethoven the agony of desecration.

Practical life, for ugly perfectionists, can be quite difficult. With trepidation I auditioned (and thankfully it was a blind one, otherwise I am sure I would not have been selected), for the second violin in the fledgling Cassiopeia Quartet, who were ambitious to make a name for themselves and escape from the lowest tier of touring troupes. The principal violin was a very handsome young man with long hair, and I bore him absolutely no malice despite his undeserved advantages; the violist, an anorexic but beautiful blonde who had just turned thirty; and the cellist a pudgy twenty-something Asian with glasses. Pudgy is being kind: she was quite heavy, but not by any means downright ugly.

I persisted despite the inevitable assault on my auditory apparatus and my principles. Frankly speaking, I needed the job.

I hope I have not given the impression that I was at all satisfied with my own playing. On the contrary I was more keenly aware of my shortcomings than anyone else, though these shortcomings were not nearly as short of the mark as those of my fellow musicians, liberally speaking.

Each rehearsal was a trial and each performance, though wildly applauded, proof of the victory of public ignorance. In quartet playing it is the custom for eye contact to occur as an aid to the timing of entries and also, to some extent, to indicate expressive changes. I had grown used to being thoroughly ignored so I simply played with eyes focussed on the score. Nevertheless I would occasionally sneak a look around and invariably I found Suzy, the cellist, doting upon the shenanigans of Emilio, the first fiddle, as he rocked and swayed and even tapped his feet. A reprehensible spectacle I stoically endured until one day, at the beginning of the second movement of Schubert's divinely sweet *Rosamunde* Quartet in A minor, I spied Emilio blowing a kiss to Suzy, who blushed, at which point I gently nudged Emilio's music stand with my foot, inducing it to topple.

Well. This caused an uproar and being ugly, the ramifications for me were unusually severe: management placed me on probation. I had three months in which to seek help and resolve my problems, problems which antedated this recent culminating act of unacceptable insolence, problems which had been noticeable since I joined them, and which included: 1) fidgeting, 2) rolling of the eyes, 3) exasperated audible sighs, 4) an indelible frown, and 5) making everyone else feel bad all the time. I put it all down to ugliness, and high ideals, a very devastating combination.

Heavy in heart I trudged off for "help" and suffered the indignities of Rolfing, the Alexander technique, Feldenkrais, yoga hot and cold, Tai Chi, pharmacopsychiatry and Cognitive Therapy, in that order. The cognitive therapist, a woolly sort of grey-haired woman who wore oversized sweaters and drank cocoa and had a beaver-like enthusiasm for positive thinking gave me homework; but no amount of visualisation would change the way I looked. It was like asking an amputee to imagine he had two legs instead of one. And to think I paid her good money! I had fortunately resisted the attempts of the psychiatrist to medicate me for "Intolerance of Imperfect Intonation," the occult syndrome he delightfully diagnosed and convinced me I had suffered from since childhood.

I was at my wits' end when an acquaintance of an acquaintance gave me a referral to someone who had helped another acquaintance, and so I found myself dubiously walking down a quiet corridor to the offices of one Dr. Sol. Scriabin was playing on CD in his waiting room, though the piano was not tuned to equal temperament, which I found QUITE curious. When Dr. Sol opened the door to greet me I looked at him, and he looked at me and I looked at him hardly believing my eyes: he was as ugly as I.

'Come in anyway,' he said.

For the first ten minutes I was speechless. How could a man this ugly achieve so much? His dog, some kind of terrier, came up and sniffed and begged to be patted.

'Go ahead, she likes you.'

Dr. Sol leaned back, with half-closed eyes as I attempted to describe my predicament.

'You're no Clark Gable,' he replied at length, 'but neither am I. However, I think I can help you. Incidentally, there is no such thing as triple "I" syndrome.'

My word! I asked him if I would have homework.

'Just show up every week and try not to be afraid of your thoughts and feelings when we speak.'

I confess that I was hardly optimistic, but as I had no other options to speak of I decided to give it a go.

So I trundled off every week to Dr. Sol's, cynically, to be honest, but punctually. His dog waited for her pats and curled up near my chair, which allowed me to stroke her ears while I tried to think of something important to say.

'Don't worry about important, just say whatever.'

So I said whatever. My probationary period was nearing an end and – and I really don't know how this was happening – the others seemed pleased with my so-called progress. What progress? I wondered. Their playing continued to rankle, as did mine.

Dr. Sol said very little during my visits, which I initially found disconcerting. He offered no advice, though occasionally he'd make a comment, such as 'Perfection is the enemy of the good.' That got me angry, and I found out later that it wasn't even original.

'It's okay to be angry: talk it out.'

Now I was really confused, but I let him have it. He took it in stride and shook my hand at the end of our session and his dog rubbed up against me as if I hadn't done anything wrong!

I kept coming weekly and I noticed that, ugly though I was, I had at least begun to enjoy the way I was thinking. Peculiar. One day, after I had gone on and on about intonation Dr. Sol asked me to come to the waiting room, where he had a Victrola. I thought it was merely a conversation piece but no, it was a functioning device. He rummaged through a stack of 78s, placed one onto the felt-covered turntable, cranked up the machine and set the needle, attached to an intricate soundbox, onto the record. It was Caruso singing an aria from *The Pearl Fishers*: "De Mon Amie."

We listened to that rough, huge and incredibly imperfect tenor voice which even broke a bit on a note. But it was... beautiful, I don't know how else to put it, beautiful, as unstoppable as an avalanche, and as warm and golden as sunlight, despite the primitive mechanism from which it issued. In this enchanting captivation I had nearly forgotten about pitch!

At our next and final session Dr. Sol with his bushy eyebrows uncharacteristically urged, 'Maybe it isn't a bad idea to strive for *im*perfection.'

I took it to heart and began to experiment on the violin, playing around the note by infinitesimal degrees. At rehearsal Emilio stilled himself and Sharon, our thin gorgeous violist, bit her lip. Suzy looked up at me and – and I smiled. Did that feel strange! It took a while for my face to recover. And somehow, quite inexplicably, their playing had ceased to irk.

On our second date Suzy confided that she had never been able to talk to anyone with such ease before.

'Even though ...' I stammered.

'Yeah, even though. Now shut up and buy me some ice cream.'

I half-winced at her coarseness until I reflected that maybe, just maybe, it was part of why I found her so darned lovely.

Violin Caprice No. 12

'Caprice: it is the essence of life! The very opposite of coercion, constriction, contraction and constraint. In short, the very opposite of marriage. Don't take me wrong. Marriage has a place, but in marriage caprice reaches its heights in the impulsive purchase of a pomegranate at the market. No, my friend, caprice cannot be bound and marriage, after all, is a contract, a contract our Doges vainly imposed on the great mother of us all, the fickle and recalcitrant sea. No doubt it is a useful tool of the state, even of value in the rearing of children, though the approach of the kibbutz is also a worthy one independent of it. Children themselves are capricious, that is, until we educate them into submission and they become servants of the straight line.'

My friend often philosophised at the Piazza San Marco where we took our coffee of an evening and witnessed the curious and absurd pageantry of pigeons and frenetic tourists, similar species, each feeding insatiably upon the crumbs of Venice, and each leaving quite a noticeable residue behind.

'There,' said Giovanni, 'that couple, do you see them? Stay still, don't turn just yet, now, two tables to your right.'

I made as if to shake the kinks out of my neck and allowed my eyes to roam in the direction he indicated.

'Typical, first time here, too old for a honeymoon, unless they are on a second marriage.'

Giovanni chuckled and shook his head.

'Not quite, my dear friend. That splendidly attractive woman is excited, excited and mildly apprehensive I believe. The ring finger of her left hand shows an untanned line. Her slightly older handsome companion, that dreamy fellow who can hardly wait to caress her, is tolerating impatiently her exhibitionism, which of course will only add to his delight later on. They are artists.'

'Artists? How can you tell?'

'Because they are obviously adulterers: she has removed her wedding band for the occasion of this assignation; he, like many men, never deigned to wear one. However, my point is that adultery is one of the highest forms of art. When properly pursued, it is the true home of caprice, the quintessence of joy. Think of it: the clandestine rendezvous, the terror of detection, the thrill of unpredictable touch, the condensation of everything notable and worthy about one-self into a caress! And of course the absence of laundry, a task that will extinguish the bravest and most dedicated passion.'

'What else can you deduce?' I mocked.

Giovanni pursed his lips. As always he was the soul of elegance in his off-white linen suit. Though seventy he looked at least ten years younger. A reliable friend, and a brilliant lawyer, married.

'Doctors, American, good at but not in love with their professions. The gentleman is a failed poet, as are all poets, and his companion a guitarist, the composer of small lyrical pieces, a mezzo-soprano.'

'Preposterous!' I exclaimed.

Giovanni laughed.

'I make my living by observing and deducing. Come, try me out.'

He called for the waiter to bring the couple drinks of their choice. They looked at us quizzically, the cue for our introduction.

'My friend Donato and I are residents of this glorious city. Permit us to welcome you. It is always a pleasure to host physicians.'

They blushed and stammered out their thanks in a curious and primitive Italian. When we returned to our table they raised their glasses.

'You see!' said Giovanni. 'And if you looked closely enough, you would have noticed the callouses on the woman's fingertips. When she spoke it was clear the voice was too low for a true soprano's. He on the other hand, aside from that look, you know, of eternal sadness in the midst of plenty, the look of horizons never to be reached, had two pens in his shirt-pocket. His coiffure is far too untidy for a surgeon's, he lacks the precision and false confidence one associates with neurology, nor does he possess the paleness of a radiologist. He must be a psychiatrist, poor man.'

'Poor man?'

'An execrable profession founded on magic and sadism.'

I understood fully.

'And she?'

'Without doubt an internist: look at the way she uses her hands, and at the softness of her face.'

How could I argue?

'They have come here to revive their dying souls. And if they are lucky enough to avoid the trap into which most adulterers fall, namely, of turning their delicious liaison into another marriage, they may yet succeed.'

I was growing tired and perhaps a bit irked by Giovanni's foolishness, so I took my leave, escaping the loud and hectic den and plunging into the labyrinthine by-ways of residential Venice to my home. I lay long upon my bed before falling asleep, Giovanni's nonsense echoing within my head and leading to this most curious dream:

I had enticed the American couple with the offer of real Venetian food and had led them to a trattoria far off the beaten track, my purpose being to test Giovanni's hypotheses. I plied them both with excellent wine and acted the genial host, hardly inquisitive, interested only in their happiness and comfort with my city. They loosened their tongues and I learned that my accursed friend had been correct in every detail! They confided in me their impossible love for one another, how they had serendipitously met a year ago at a conference and discovered their common interest in the poetic and musical arts and thereafter hazarded secret rendezvous to share pleasures of the flesh and soul, and how, although their marriages were more congenial because they demanded so much less of their spouses, now here in Venice they wished to resolve whether they should forsake their families and marry each other, swearing not to leave the city before a decision had been made. They looked upon me as the heavenly-sent arbitrator who held their fate in his hands and they awaited my pronouncement.

Before I could respond a violinist appeared at our table to offer a serenade. She was dark and lithe, a gypsy, with slender and alluring arms. Her blouse shimmered and occasionally fell in such a way upon her breasts to reveal her beauties. We accepted her offer and she played music of exquisite yearning, doleful, sweet, and – capricious! Her tempi shifted unpredictably, the moods she limned varied without warning and she seemed the very embodiment of impulsive wayward love. I whispered to her that we had a musician in our midst and she invited the American woman to play. The woman demurred, claiming the absence of a guitar as an excuse, but the gypsy brought her to her feet and handed her the fiddle. While demonstrating how to hold the instrument, her body pressed lightly against the American's and for a moment she placed her hand upon her waist. She instructed her to hold her fingers in a stationary position on the strings and, standing behind her, took her right hand in her own and guided the bow. A simple melody came forth, rich and wistful,, and the small crowd of diners applauded. The gypsy disappeared but not before turning frankly towards the woman as if summoning her with her wild glowing eyes.

Sensing catastrophe I began to lecture, on love. The American man was pale and the woman now vacant, but I persisted, drawing upon Ovid, Plutarch and Dante, and concluding that coercion, of any kind, meant the death of love. Love must be free, utterly and completely, I asserted. It must be capricious! Only adulterous love could be true love. I advised them both to rid themselves of their ignorant superstitions, to remain married to their spouses, and to pursue their private passion without expectations of the other, or plan. Tossing my napkin to the table, I rose and bade them good night. They appeared rooted, unmoved, unlistening.

To work off the feverish excitement of the evening I walked circuitously home until I was stopped in my tracks by a tune wafting down the waterway: the very melody played together by the gypsy and the American. I hastened toward its source, round and round about, crossing and criss-crossing the canals but it receded, elusively out of reach for what seemed an eternity, and I at last ran out of breath, not certain where I could be. Just at that point a shout from several gondoliers arose and I peered down and saw that the limp body of a man was being fished from the warm placid water. It was the American! They

pointed up at me, raised their fists and issued a cry of alarm. I
retreated in horror and fled but, because I was already fatigued
from my quest for the music, collapsed at the church of San Ger-
emia with the mob on my heels.

I woke late, dressed hurriedly and stopped for a coffee. At
the bar I glanced at the newspaper and saw that a drown-
ing had occurred not far from the Rio dei Fuseri, a foreigner.
Beads of sweat began to form on my brow, despite my better judgment. I inquired further: an American. My cup fell
from my fingers and Matteo, the barman chuckled as if to say
'That's what you get for a night on the town!' He winked and
I threw him my coins, hastening to Giovanni's offices.

'Did you hear?'

'About?'

'The American, the one who drowned, the one we met,
the adulterer! The poet-doctor, the doctor-poet, whoever,
the artist,' I babbled, 'he's dead just as in my dream!'

I related the dream, incoherently, and Giovanni placed his
arm around my shoulders and eased me onto a chair.

He then wisely brought me a drink and I confessed everything to him, how for the past two years I had carried on
with an enchanting musician, part-gypsy, whose art and
body were irresistible, and how the affair had turned from
a galvanising romp into the most execrable of tortures, for I
had become jealous to the point of mania, unable to abide
her absence, unable to contemplate the attentions she would
receive when she played, and unable to endure my wife's pettiness, for which reason I had recently taken a flat. I told him
that I had begged her to leave her good-for-nothing lout of
a husband, the brute whom she slept beside, even if chastely.

And then I told him the worst of it all, that I had refused her a child, which she had begged of me, unless she divorced.

Giovanni regarded me with pity.

'You are no artist, my friend. You have destroyed the capriciousness of love with your insane conventionality.'

'Help me, Giovanni, what am I to do?'

'It is very simple. What kind of musician is your lover?'

'A violinist, curse her.'

'You must write to her and tell her that you are taking the air in Treviso as an escape from Venice's putrid summer. And that you will send her some amusing missives.'

I was incredulous, and frantic.

'What? Leave her to find another lover in my absence?'

'She is more likely to take a lover the harder you press. Now, listen to me. Go to Treviso. Take up the pen, forsake that silly poetic nonsense you are drawn to, and write her things that are funny, not too long, things that are ... capricious, and that include the violin. Am I clear? And whatever you do, do not let the gypsy visit you in Treviso. In fact, better to send the stories to me: I will pass them on so she won't be able to track you down. When you have written a dozen of them, you will make a triumphant return to Venice, okay? And I repeat: be light and witty, toss them off and don't belabour them as you do your gloomy verse. I will also go to your wife and reassure her that you love her, that the children are your soul, that you realise you were mad to have left and that you have undertaken psychiatric treatment to make you whole again. Go! Go! Have some fun!'

Easier said than done, I thought ruefully.

'And by the way,' he added, 'That couple. They were Canadian. Pharmacists. Married. She plays ukulele. The American they found in the canal – a drunken simpleton who attempted to leap onto a departing vaporetto after an angry girlfriend.'

And so I did as advised. It required all my strength to stay put and to start composing these miniatures. It was at first like wading through Venetian mud, but with application I managed to achieve a degree of levity and marvelled at the distance between these little pieces and my serious poetic work. As soon as I completed a story I posted it to Giovanni, who in turn promised to deliver it on my behalf, retaining a copy for himself as a matter of interest. After I had penned the final tale, I felt lighter, buoyant, and serene, a Caesar prepared for a procession.

Imagine my shock when back in Venice I discovered that my wife had filed for divorce and my lover was pregnant, by her spouse, or so she said.

'Giovanni! Giovanni! How could you? I am wretched, ruined beyond hope!' I exclaimed, having burst into his rooms.

The lawyer, bless him, was unfazed. He brought out two glasses of brandy. I gulped mine straightaway with trembling hands. Giovanni's avuncular reassurance calmed.

'What are you worried about? No small-minded wife, no demanding lover! And these,' he said, waving my manuscripts in his hand, 'you're a free man, Donato, you capricious son of a bitch! Go write another twelve!'

He laughed, and I laughed, we both laughed, and in our growing and roaring unpent laughter toasted "caprice".

'To caprice! Caprice! Down with conventionality! Up with caprice! Caprice!'

We laughed and drank and laughed some more. 'To caprice!' I shouted, kicking my heels and whirling clumsily about.

'I'll say this, Donato,' said Giovanni at length, wiping away his mirthful tears, 'those women are something else.'

It was the way he said "something else" that brought my capers to a halt and sent a creeping shudder through my spine. My mind was spinning. My friend – was he my friend? – merely shrugged his eyebrows as if to say 'Life is inherently comic.'

Ha. Ah. Oh well. To caprice?

To caprice!

Violin Caprice No. 13

It wasn't a rule that poets needed to be so ill-dressed, but more like a law. Women poets with ample charms disguised them and men with few simply became completely charmless. At his first reading my friend Jasper Jones made the mistake of apparelling himself in reasonably well-fitting and fashionable garb. The other mistake was insisting on the nom-de-plume "Casper Sarcophagus." He corrected the first quickly enough, but, being stubborn continued to hide his light under the kind of bushel only a stray dog would sniff. And no matter what anybody says about a rose smelling sweet whatever you call it, the same cannot be said for a poet whose surname is "Sarcophagus." I tried to tell him but you know what poets are like: poetic. He had good reasons, he said, to juxtapose the empty levity of popular culture, which I took to mean "Casper," with the covert truth of human mortality, adding something about a husk enveloping the hollow of the modern spirit before I glazed over. I tried to tell him that George Gordon, Lord Byron, otherwise known to the poetic world as "Byron" – simple, strong and Byronic (he didn't even chuckle) would not have cut the mustard if he sprouted verse under a by-line like "Charlie Cheesewheel." But hey, at the end of the day it's his call.

The harder part for me was weighing in on the "effluvia of a feverishly inspired brain," that is, his poems, as he often referred to them.

'Gary, I've outdone myself this time. Take a look.' He handed me a raggedly torn piece of notebook paper with a barely legible scrawl requiring translation.

'Why don't you type them out?' I pleaded.

'That comes later. This is creativity's first blush.'

Once I had read the thing, never more than a dozen lines, unrhymed ('rhyme has totalitarian roots,' he asserted), I puzzled over its meaning.

'Don't worry about meaning, Gary, poems aren't meant to *mean*, get it, but to *be*.'

That sounded vaguely familiar but I still felt as if I were missing something. Nevertheless I usually came up with a pensive nod and an adjective like "vivid" or "expressive" or "moving". Occasionally "wow."

'Very few people understand the sweat that goes into poetry. It took me four hours to decide on that comma – but it works.'

Four hours of a beautiful Saturday morning.... At least now, after these Herculean labours, he'd come to the beach and ogle the girls. More material for the feverish brain, apparently, since the main source of his inspiration was unrequited love, which he had in spades. And since there's nothing like unrequited love to stimulate a thirst for drink, at least we would have a good night of it afterwards.

Fortunately Jasper had a day job to support the poetic habit: accountancy (as a smithy of words he insisted on the British variant over the dull American "accounting"). We were colleagues in fact, but whereas Jasper saw his day job as a necessary evil I merely saw it as necessary. Neither of us obviously fit the mould, he being poetic and I being, well, a bit of rebel myself, often organising karaoke junkets for the office. He wasn't a big fan of them, but we had a quid pro quo with the poetry readings. To tell the truth I thought it might be a good place to meet women who didn't work with numbers, which I was desperate to do because the numbers gals tended to be a bit pinched and more than a tad boring: for example, they hardly ever came to karaoke.

Round about our fifth or sixth excursion to the dingy basement café where the readings were held, Casper blazoned his latest:

> Music of no words
> have you brought, laughing
> to me

Yep, that was it. I mention it because it was easy to remember, being short, because the comma required several sleepless nights, and because it ties in to transpiring events. After Jasper bathed in the sparse but audible applause a thin willowy girl walked slowly to the makeshift stage. She carried a fiddle but no bow. When she reached the microphone – and all you could see of her basically was a pale oval face framed by big dark hair, a petite Yoko Ono – she raised the violin and plucked the strings harshly, extended her arms and let out a wail. A very long wail. A wail that went on for about three minutes by my watch, interspersed with gasps for breath, and concluding with another pluck.

I vowed that this would be my last venture and I was working up to telling Jasper when he turned to me with a kind of 'My god!' look and said 'My god!'

'My god is right,' I replied.

We waited for the rest of the smithies to exhaust the Muse so Jasper could approach the wailer who, despite the moxie of her performance, turned out to be a shy thing. I stayed put and watched their heads bobbing, saw Jasper wrench out his scrap, gesticulate, lean forward in that earnest way of his, and nod pensively, pensive nods being quite the thing around poetry, when she lifted the fiddle. They were both smiling the kinds of smiles you couldn't cut with a knife because they were so gooey, and by the time he got back to me he was a Jasper to be reckoned with.

'Gary,' he beamed, 'this is no coincidence. You heard my poem. Then *she* comes on: the living *realisation* of it, which she realised *subconsciously*. And the violin. Come on, now tell me about the pseudonym, tell me if that's a coincidence too!'

I didn't get his drift.

'Sarcophagus! The violin itself is a sarcophagus, literally – of sound that dies – and metaphorically.'

'How do you mean metaphorically?'

'It contains dead sound.'

'But I thought that was literal.'

'That's just it! The convergence of the two in the one! Look, Gary, I come in and read my poem about wordless music. Me, *Casper Sarcophagus*. She comes in and she *gives* us wordless music, and uses a literal/metaphorical *sarcophagus* to do so. Now do you get it? This was meant to be. Besides, I've got her number.'

I thought calling an eerie scream music was a bit of a stretch but I kept it to myself.

I didn't see much of either Jasper or Casper outside work, where my buddy was paying far more attention to commas than decimal points. He spent lunchtime on the phone and at five on the dot he would rush out like a character in search of a long-lost author who would punish him for being late to the reunion. In short, they were an item. Whenever he came up for air out of the poetic soup, which wasn't often, all he could do was babble on and on about Miranda, whose pseudonym was Caliban, and when he said "Caliban" a quiet reflective frisson of boundless admiration shimmered over his mooning face. Luckily she couldn't get over "Sarcophagus" for sheer irony.

'Gary,' he confessed, 'she's an artist. I try, but she succeeds. It's a privilege but at the same time an incredible onus.'

He munched on a celery stalk, a new habit encouraged by the artist.

'The great consolation is that I can but strive. And really, that's all anyone can do.'

Before I could reply to this casually-revealed but profound truth he hurriedly pulled a few spreadsheets across the desk to conceal his heap of literary excursions as the boss approached.

Artists, even *I* knew, have temperaments. I suppose it's the price of admission. I'll explain.

Jasper was going on about a collaborative performance he and Miranda were planning, the trick of which was how to marry his words to her wordlessness. While ironing out the kinks they were both keen to get my "outsider" opinion. I took a deep breath but agreed to give it my all, promising myself that a big "wow" was the least I could do in return for private and exclusive dinner theatre.

By vegan standards the meal might have clocked in as adequate, but for any self-respecting sybarite it was a washout. Jasper, who was known to revel in the mass-produced mush served for *hoi polloi* on the New Jersey turnpike, picked at his pickings without betraying the slightest dismay. Miranda

served a non-alcoholic so-called wine, adding injury to the
insulted, but Jasper quaffed as if it were ambrosia. No wonder she was so thin.

'We'll hold off dessert until after our little – what shall
we call it honey? A demonstration, or a performance? I like
demonstration, the Greekness of the word.'

Yep, it was all Greek to me, I thought, girding myself.

'I'll fetch the sarcophagus,' she quipped, flashing a flirta-
tious eye, and Jasper showed all the world, which at the time
consisted of Miranda and myself, that he had thirty-two of
the whitest.

I'll say this, she had a certain way about her, a wispy allure
with a titanium underbelly: a fetching but tough cookie.
Obviously Jasper's type.

Having returned with the prop, she gave Jasper his cue
and he began, the usual drivel about evanescence, death, the
loss of love, frivolous hope, the insufficiency of words, etc.,
though I noted he was far more wordy than ever. Inspired
perhaps. Then in the midst of a crescendo of sighing expos-
tulation, Miranda, who had been plucking away in the background on the sarcophagus, broke in with one of her pat-
ented shrieks. If you've ever seen a runaway train, which I
haven't, you'll get a feel for Caliban's commitment: basically
unstoppable. Only Caliban was off the tracks. Casper meanwhile couldn't hear himself, so he gently reached out to his
partner in art, who seemed flustered by the interruption, for
her eyes, the better no doubt to concentrate on the yodel,
had been shut.

'Darling, I think it might be a bit too loud.' She was
shaken.

'I just meant that it was getting hard for me to hear myself,
honey.'

I fully expected her to show a bit of annoyance but ultimately to pull up the bootstraps and plunge once more unto the breach after she had cooled her heels. Instead, she left the room precipitously, Jasper now having to do whatever breaching on his own in pursuit. He returned, pale and uncomfortable. Miranda followed after a brief eternity with dessert, one scoop of sugar- and fat-free organic soy ice-cream containing a cream substitute, which she set down with surprising force for one her size.

We ate – if one could call ingesting a flavourless chemical confection eating – in complete silence. A tempestuous silence, in fact.

'Well, Gary,' inquired my hostess at length, 'what did you think of the collaboration? Aside from the fact that the collaborators were apparently on *different wavelengths*, did you get anything out of it?'

Something about her tone, and particularly the crispness with which she took care to enunciate "different wavelengths," told me that a mere "wow" would not, under the circumstances, suffice. So I became a bit more fulsome, spewing out a garbled version of the literal and metaphorical connections between the violin and my friend's pseudonymous surname.

'What's in a name? Everything. And nothing. A rose is sweet. Sounds die. That's the music of it. Brilliant.'

Jasper, out of the corner of my eye, was cringing while Miranda – well, I think "seethed" is the best way to describe it. And then all of a sudden she laughed, a bit high-pitched, but it qualified, and the tension in the air that only a chain-saw could make a dent in relaxed, like a bomb successfully defused. I joined in, and Jasper began to chuckle, and the three of us all seemed so relieved that Miranda had us holding hands round the table for "post-grace" and I was about to break into Kumbaya.

Miranda asked to see Jasper's poem, and he coughed it up, all two sheets, quite proudly. She perused the ode, smiled ever so sweetly and then ceremoniously ripped the papers into very small pieces, which she stuffed through the sound holes of her violin.

Jasper was not happy. He became even less happy when she set the papers alight and told him that one sarcophagus deserved another.

We left together, posthaste, urged to exit the premises by Miranda's Caliban-like vocal apparatus.

Jasper was a combination of downcast, disheartened, despondent and disconsolate, all in one, like a famished anteater in Antarctica, and even a psychologist could see he needed bucking up. I had an idea.

Several hours later I had to pry him off the stage of *Rick's Mecca*, where they're still talking about his rendition of "That'll Be the Day," his consumption of five "Big Burgers," and the knockout with a reputation as a flat-out tease who accompanied him home.

And me? I'm relishing accountancy, especially now that I can share my passion with an investment banker.

Violin Caprice No. 14

Although I hadn't seen Professor Eisenman in over two years, when his summons came I responded immediately, despite my misgivings. He was at the best of times a difficult soul: ornery, dictatorial, cantankerous, irascible and mercurial. But unarguably a great, and I mean *great*, musician. I suppose I loved him more than I hated him, but not by much.

I had started lessons with him at the Conservatory in my teens and then, after I got my orchestra gig, saw him on and off for years. He once threw a chair at me during a session to catch my attention. And on another occasion he walked out of the practice room whilst I was lost in my own marvellous interpretation of the Tchaikovsky concerto: it took me a good ten minutes to figure out he wasn't there. At least he didn't charge me for that one. I pushed back when I could. He was forever advocating the execution of the beginning of the Sibelius without vibrato, despite my protests, and at my graduation recital I laid it on thick, the vibrato that is, which is how I liked it then. We began speaking again several months later: he even congratulated me for having the guts to parade my poor taste in public.

He was a most unconventional man, and teacher. For a whole year he had me play without a chin-rest and on gut strings, even the E! It was a way, he stressed, for me to know how my predecessors struggled. 'Ontogeny recapitulates phylogeny!' he cryptically exclaimed. He also had very strong interpretative opinions though, to be fair, he entertained dissent when alternatives were thoughtfully presented. Thus did I earn his respect, for I always marshalled cogent rationales. Naturally his technical pointers were invaluable and have certainly contributed to my considerable success as a violinist, but when I pressed him for more transcendent advice, being ambitious, he responded as follows:

1. do more than just music
2. don't take yourself too seriously, and
3. if love comes calling always open the door, no matter what, no matter what

Coming from him that second point was a bit rich, and as for number three I suspected it was his way of justifying the numerous messy affairs he conducted.

We all know the kind of violinist he was: superb, highly individualistic, with a magnificent tone. He was wise enough to retire at his meridian, before arthritis could interfere with the attainment of his lofty ideals. I understand that at his farewell recital of unaccompanied works, he played *all* of Paganini's *Caprices* as an encore, every single one of them, and modestly remarked, 'That's about as good as it gets.' His audience of peers seemed to agree. Thereafter he taught actively at the Conservatory which is where I first met him, larger than life and nearly always embroiled in a scandal. Let's just say he had a hard time keeping male friends.

While in his mid-seventies a student one-third his age (sic!) moved in; when she left a year later it was not because the Dean came begging him for the sake of the school's already precarious moral reputation but because she began to bore the Professor with overweening ambition, lack of discipline, and, most unforgivably, an airy and hollow tone, so he threw her out. He was known around town for wearing a cape and using a cane, which given his Austrian background weren't affectations.

To be fair the man could also be most generous, with his knowledge and with his violins, having donated both his Stradivarius *and* Guarnerius to the Smithsonian ('probably replicas made by Vuillaume,' he scoffed), although he retained his instrument of choice, the beloved Amati. He allowed me to play on it a number of times and I don't care what anybody says, that damned violin made me sound like a god. I knew he had grown fond of me when he suggested that I drop the "Professor" when addressing him: 'No need to be so formal: *Mr*. Eisenman will do.' I appreciated the gesture but could never break the habit.

He married for the first time two years ago, at the ripe young age of seventy-nine and I had been excluded from the ceremony, having apparently taken some grave musical liberty with which he strenuously disagreed while soloing in *Scheherazade*, or so rumour had it. I left the ball in his court. It came as a relief after all this time to hear from him again: perhaps it was for the apology I so thoroughly deserved!

At the Professor's home I was greeted by a woman dressed in black, mid-thirties, I guessed, who disappeared with my coat. Rather pretty for a house-servant, though a bit severe and not quite as deferential as I would have expected, but there you are.

The Professor entered and we shook hands. He looked old; well, he *was* old; but he also looked uncommonly feeble and this came as a shock. 'Have you met my wife?' he asked.

'No, just the maid.'

'We don't have a maid. That was Mrs. Eisenman.'

'I beg your pardon, Professor,' I responded with chagrin as she reappeared.

'It's quite all right. Mrs. Eisenman, Mr. Schwarz, a fine instrumentalist. Now, come with me.'

The Professor led me to his study which was filled to the rafters with books. He was a polymath and it showed. He offered a chair and asked whether I wished a drink. How could I refuse his exceptional brandy? He made not the slightest reference to the rift he had instigated, which of course was typical.

'Now then, Mr. Schwarz. I have a great favour to ask of you. But first, tell me, how is life? Not the orchestra, but life itself: are you still a bachelor?'

I confessed as much.

'And why is that?'

'Well, you know, I still haven't found the right one I guess.'

'At your age there's no rush.'

'I suppose not.'

The inquisition was already beginning to irk me.

'And your playing? You continue to give the odd recital, chamber works, etc.?'

'Yes, sure, it keeps me going, though I very much enjoy the orchestra.'

I was in fact a rarity: a concertmaster who really and thoroughly loved his job. I revelled in the sumptuous sound of strings all round me, in the antics of conductors good and ill, which made for tragicomic diversion, in my motley colleagues with their infantile gripes and not-so-secret intrigues. And whereas many complained about repetition in the repertoire I gloried in it as an opportunity to experiment and grow. I awaited an allusion to Rimsky-Korsakov, but none came.

'How are the orchids? I hear you have become quite the horticulturalist.'

I chuckled and told him of the delight I continued to glean from the cultivation of these splendid flowers. That was the thing about him: he was genuinely interested, and he could elicit and show such human warmth and kindness that I nearly always forgave him his trespasses against what I deeply believed to be a friendship.

'I have a proposition to make. I have been informed by my physicians that I have approximately three to six months to live. Please, no sentimentality. I have had a full and reward-ing life, but there is something I wish to accomplish before I leave this vale.'

The news put my grievances into perspective and my flesh became leaden as I thought of my own inevitable demise.

'Take advantage of the brandy, Mr. Schwarz. There, now, good. I have made arrangements. Mrs. Eisenman of course will assist, but as she is a composer she must not be distracted overmuch from her creative work, which is paramount. I am already taking up enough of her time.'

He paused for a moment and added frankly, as he would when we freely and hotly debated musical ideas, 'She believes that Schoenberg was too melodic in his late works.'

I kept a straight face.

'However,' he qualified, 'she has many endearing qualities.'

I nearly spat out a mouthful of brandy and had to disguise my mirth with a cough.

'I would like to bequeath my Amati to you, Mr. Schwarz. Would you do it justice?'

'Professor!'

'But there are conditions. Are you touring extensively this year?'

'No, we'll be here mostly, just two weeks away, and I can probably get out of that.'

He regarded me keenly.

'You are a good man even though your musical decisions have at times tested my patience. There, take the instrument and play something, Goldmark's *Air*.'

On the Amati I felt I had been given new and wondrously expressive abilities. The Professor nodded approvingly.

'Now then, Mr. Schwarz, here is what I propose.'

And so the master laid out his request. He wished to compose an autobiographical memoir but required a reliable hand: me. He wished furthermore for his wife and me to vet each chapter together as a safeguard and perhaps offer suggestions, which he being the author had a right to disregard. Could I spare several hours a week for the next several months? It would mean the world to him. If that lickspittle and fool Dittersdorf could do it – dictate an autobiography – so surely could he, with my help. A publisher had already been engaged. Like Hamlet, he said, he wished his cause to be reported aright. Don't we all, I mused.

I was deeply touched but I told him bluntly that I would under no circumstances, *none whatsoever*, accept the Amati for my efforts. It took a full hour of wrangling for him to persuade me, and I was won over only when he threatened to smash the instrument, which he had extricated from its case and now held poised in the air, on the corner of his desk if I persisted in my foolish stubbornness.

'One more refusal, Mr. Schwarz, and no one, believe me, no one, will get the Amati!' he declared.

What could I do?

He called his wife into the study and outlined our schedule. Saturday mornings he would dictate directly to me on computer, and Wednesday evenings his wife and I would review the draft. He seemed sincerely apologetic for the demands on my time but I assured him that it was really and truly the greatest of privileges and the least I could do. The Professor waved a dismissive hand. When I inquired about the nature of his illness he brushed me off, asserting that whatever happened he would never allow diapers or bedpans in his life. I was almost tempted to embrace him when we parted, but thought better of it and merely shook his hand.

As his wife met me at the door with my coat she smiled wryly.

'Thank you, Mr. Schwarz. He has spoken warmly of you.'

I arrived the next weekend, laptop in hand.

'Good morning, Mr. Schwarz.'

'Please call me Nathan,' I responded, 'and your name is ... '

'*Mrs. Eisenman.*'

So much for the genial first step. A steely beauty, just what the Professor deserved.

'My husband is waiting.'

The Professor set to work without ado and if I had been expecting wonders and revelations, they were not forthcoming, nor was much in the way of personal detail. He named his parents, which for him appeared to be saying a lot, and spoke in the most skeletal manner of his musical upbringing. I emailed the transcript to Mrs. Eisenman and on the following Wednesday we had our first meeting to discuss the material. There was, however, very little to discuss, though I did learn, in a perfunctory kind of way, about the recent accidental diagnosis of advanced lymphoma and the Professor's refusal to undergo palliative treatment.

The Saturdays and Wednesdays proceeded apace, and it became quickly apparent that "autobiography" was a term

that could hardly be justified for his dictations. "Meandering meditation" might better describe what turned out to
be extended and unpredictable musings about the works of
the greater and lesser Romantic composers, full of technical explication and concentrating quite specifically on interpretative approaches. Whenever his wife or I suggested the
slightest alteration he invoked authorial rights to refuse.
Though his mental faculties remained sharp and he was not
in any discernible pain, his physical decline was striking.

The haggard and anguished Mrs. Eisenman however
seemed strangely enough more attractive – or perhaps not so
strangely, as suffering can soften. Once we had despatched the
most recent chapter she let the facade drop a bit and we each
reflected on the great man who remained ensconced in his
study as we deliberated, out of respect for the privacy which
the task he imposed required. I spoke of the terror of my first
meeting with him, of my frantic preparations to impress and
of the greatest joy I had when he picked up the fiddle to demonstrate a point. She seemed to relish the very small things
I remembered, his unheralded acts of kindness, the volcanic
but impersonal outbursts of temper, and the inviolably genuine seriousness he brought to our art. Humour, however,
was not his strong suit, nor for that matter did it seem to be
hers. Somehow or other I got to speaking about myself, my
parents' poverty and my incessant childhood scuffles on the
street; the imposition of the violin upon me to keep me out
of trouble; and the great and easy progress I had made on the
instrument I gradually grew to love.

The old man appeared unexpectedly at the door.

'Movina, I require your help.'

So that was her name!

On the spur of the moment I decided to give Movina one of my orchids, a precious and beautiful specimen which she received with spontaneous delight before reverting to form. I was glad to bring some measure of cheer to attenuate the heavy gloom that was unavoidable at the home.

She however remained an enigma. What did she expect from the Professor as a husband, what *could* she expect from anyone his age, no matter how formidable or brilliant? What was wrong with her?

I've never met a composer who didn't think that a good hundred hours of animated discussion about his or her latest composition wasn't living life to the full, so I let slip a few asides and she took the bait. Would I care to see what she was working on? Of course! It might, I hoped, provide a few clues. But when I reviewed the score I was unmoved: the music was dreadfully arcane, dreary and mechanically mathematical, a hodgepodge of post-modernist atonal drivel.

On Saturday as the Professor came up for air from a long passage on the Smetana quartet (the man had stamina even in illness!), he remarked that he wished Movina would take a leaf out of the Czech's book, so to speak, that she had a gift for melody and that she was inherently a miniaturist. He also added that she was allergic to dishonesty, but what this had to do with melody and miniaturism eluded me. Then he resumed.

I dreaded the following Wednesday, when she was sure to ask my opinion. Despite the Professor's condition and its emotional demands she seemed less careworn than before. She encouraged me through my hesitation to give a full and most honest opinion of her composition: which I summed up by saying that I found the music, well, sterile. In hindsight I can't fathom a more tactless choice of terms. I braced for anger, cool or hot, but not tears, not from her; but it was tears that came, flowing in abundance, tears not only about her artistic shortcomings, but about the dying man who had been so magnanimous and the deaths of her own parents when she was a youth; tears about a future that now held nothing but emptiness. The frailty of her became manifest, and with it a glimpse into her character, a glimpse that her music sought to conceal. I don't know what possessed me, but when I reached out and took her hand in my own to comfort and atone, she did not withdraw.

That simple act of consolation proved not to be so simple at all: it catalysed an obsessive tumult that instantly overtook me, body and soul. She was astonishingly alluring, I finally admitted to myself, despite – or because of? – the pains she took to be a cold-hearted bitch. And distressingly irresistible. How much longer could I endure this charade? But how could I stop?

Saturday proved excruciating as the lustreless wearying eyes of the Professor seared into my hypocritical skull. He had suddenly and inexplicably decided on a new tack: a catalogue of his amatory exploits. I blushed for Movina as I faithfully transcribed his highly personal treatise on infidelity and conquest, and the following Wednesday, when she greeted me with a fleeting impulsive embrace in thanks for the gift of another orchid, the pressure, slight as it was, of her body along the deprived length of my own, sent me into a dreadful ecstasy. She pretended to be unfazed by the Professor's latest installation and I did my best to preserve a stoic and aloof demeanour. I made a few brief desultory and inane remarks in conclusion as Movina accompanied me to the threshold.

I took her hand with every intention of quickly departing, but when she pressed mine in return, it became simply
impossible not to kiss, and not to kiss again, passionately,
wonderfully, heedlessly, over and over, to hold that lithe
graceful figure in my arms, to feel impetuous reckless recip-
rocal desire, and more, while all that glorious while the
wretched cancer-ridden image of my artistic father plagued
the shreds and patches of my better self.

The next weekend I was a bundle of uncontrollably
excited nerves. I accepted a brandy from Movina, equally
agitated, whom the Professor peremptorily and, I thought,
rather harshly dismissed. Had she told him?

'Mr. Schwarz, I am beginning to experience pain. The
kind of pain I have never felt before.'

I bowed my head in shame and was about to blurt out
who knows what when he checked me.

'I do not wish to die in agony so I have informed my physician that I am ready. But I would like to tell you something.
Do me the courtesy of hearing me out in full.'

I spilled half the contents of my snifter, trembling
uncontrollably.

'Your services are no longer necessary for the
autobiography.'

Now crimson with self-loathing I tried to sink as deeply as
possible into the cushions of my seat, lowering my eyes.

'It was a ruse.'

A pause. I looked up.

He smiled. Ghastly, even ghostly, but there was no mistake: a smile.

'It was the only way you could come to know one another,
you and Movina. Men must endure their going hence, even as

their coming hither. You have opened the door and become a man. It's about time.'

Son of a bitch.

At the funeral two weeks later, I played the *Air* from Goldmark's concerto in A minor on the marvellous Amati he had bequeathed. And, in accordance with the Professor's meticulously stipulated testament, that very *Air* served as a prelude to the vows of marriage Movina and I pledged immediately thereafter.

As for miniatures, why we now have one of flesh and blood lying right between us. Movina composes serenades for her, serenades that are most decidedly tonal, I am happy to say, and deliciously melodic.

Violin Caprice No. 15

Sean concluded in the dark that New Zealand was no place to be crazy. He thought he was in prison, given the cardboard bedpan, paper cups with water, inch-thick vinyl-covered foam "mattress" on a hard cold floor, a small window hung on its outside with yellowed bedcloth, and the locked door, against which he banged. Okay, he knew he'd gotten a little out of hand and as he rummaged through his memory for the causal chain that led to his predicament in the here and now, it was as if instead of the full suit of clothes he'd managed only half a shirt and a sock. In other words, he was still too out of it to think straight.

Just then the "curtain" over the window rippled and he backed into a corner, scared as hell. Where was his fiddle? Where the hell was his violin? He searched frantically in his cell, even lifting the so-called mattress, and he started to yell, kicking the walls and door with his bare feet (where were his shoes?) until the curtain rippled again, a grating sound was heard in the lock of the door and six big people, male and female, entered. Before he could explain himself he was face-down, his arms pinned, and he felt a sharp jab in his right buttock. The mob disappeared as quickly as they had entered and he sat, cross-legged on the floor, too stunned to cry and too weak to mobilise his limbs.

Morning did bring clarity. Alright, he had cut loose at a party nine-thousand miles from the East Coast, figuring he could get away with a little recklessness so far from home. And yeah, he'd had a few joints and a few too many beers, and then ... and then, yes, he began to remember, the light fixtures were spying on him and whispering and he tried to tell people about it and he started to run, brandishing his fiddle, because they were going to kill him, PLEASE HELP! Next came prison or, as he was astonished to learn, the hospital.

This was a hospital? He heard noises outside his cell so he shouted. No response. Then all of a sudden a big fat slovenly guy appeared in the doorway. 'Keep that up and you'll get another jab,' he threatened. His accent was Irish. Eventually a doctor materialised. Neither he nor the nurses wore anything that would identify them as professionals except for a dangling nametag.

'Where's my violin?' he demanded, 'where's my violin?'

He refused to reply to anything until they answered his question, so they removed themselves and locked the door.

By the third day of seclusion he had been broken, so he played ball. They promised to let him out gradually, but only if he could demonstrate self-control. Biting his tongue, his lip and his brain, he conceded, and freedom beckoned – freedom being a small corridor where five or six other patients roamed about begging for cigarettes from the nursing station, a tiny fortress at the corridor's end. Otherwise like him they remained sequestered in solitary confinement, shouting from time to time, vainly.

Sean had read enough of Kafka to know that this wasn't good. There was a courtyard to which patients, the compliant ones, the well-behaved, had access. He entered. It was tiny but at least there was light, finally. Sitting at a picnic table and smoking his brains out was a big brown fellow with a weird tattoo on his face and tattoos over his massive arms. He offered him a smoke, which Sean declined.

'Not from here, are you bro?'

'No, I'm from New York.'

'The Yankees!'

'Yeah. Hey, I'm Sean,' said the violinist, extending his hand. The brown guy rose and before the startled Sean could even think to flee had pressed his forehead and nose against his. But he wasn't hurt and the brown guy asked him to sit down. Joseph, he learned, was Maori which to New Zealanders was what the Indians were to Americans. Again, probably not good. Joseph didn't seem crazy, but Sean was wary.

'Nah, bro, I smoked a little too much dack.'

'Like me!' They laughed.

'When do we get out?' asked Sean.

'I'm looking at tomorrow. I hate being in lock-up here: prison's better. Act nice when they give you the medicine but stick it up your cheek and when they turn away spit it out. The shit's poison, believe me.'

The fat Irishman appeared and ordered Sean back to his room.

'But I just got out.'

'Let's start over again: go to your room, mate.'

A menacing asshole, thought Sean, who obeyed. Joseph went on smoking, but lifted his eyebrows twice, rapidly. Because of his outburst the night before, Sean was told, he would be in the Intensive Care Unit for a week. If he behaved himself they would allow him onto the Open Side. So that's where he was, the Intensive Care Unit. Some care. He pleaded for the violin.

'Ask the doctor.'

'Where is he? Can I see him now?'

'He'll be around tomorrow. Now let's get back in.'

The human spirit adapts astonishingly well to coercion and fear. Sean became docile. Joseph, he noted, didn't. He shouted for his rights and the goon squad appeared, this time reinforced by security guards, and Joseph was thrown – quite literally – into his cell, after an injection had been administered. It took two days of quiet for him to get out and Sean caught up with him in the courtyard again. He really didn't seem nuts, whereas the others now wandering around muttered to themselves and looked woefully forlorn and dishevelled, like the inmates at the asylum in the movie *Amadeus*.

The doctor arrived, a heavy-set man with a lupine snout and a European accent he couldn't quite place. He agreed to allow Joseph his violin, but without the strings. Precautions.

'What do you mean without the strings? What good is it without the damned strings? And no, I'm not suicidal, you jerk! I just want to play my damn fiddle!' Sean was shouting. Not good.

'Jerry, get the orderlies,' called the doctor.

That night while stewing in seclusion Sean, whose ears were very finely attuned, heard some interesting sounds from the direction of the nursing station. A slit in the curtain showed him what he suspected, and as the woman rose to her feet he moved away from the window. Next day in the courtyard he told Joseph, who merely shrugged.

'They're animals, nothing new. I need to get out, bro.'

'Just be good for a few days, alright? They promised me I could leave.'

'You're white, bro, it's different with us Maori. You see that girl there? She's been here for six months. Yeah, she's crazy, but six months, bro ... nobody's *that* crazy. Except this place can make you that way. They inject her every week, every damned week.'

And Joseph tried to tell the young American about his people, about a certain treaty that was lost and found, about calculated exploitation, about how the Maori had nearly become extinct like a big flightless bird that once roamed the land of the long white cloud, about the language that was suppressed and now about what he called window-dressing – using Maori ceremonies to make Kiwis – no, not the fruit, the colonials who thought they ruled the earth and sea and sky – look like they care.

'So you're like all the Blacks in the States.'

'You know about the All Blacks?'

'Yeah, all the Blacks are treated like you guys.'

'Huh?'

It was hard for Sean to follow, but he understood one thing exceptionally clearly: Joseph was going to lose it if they kept him locked up much longer. He was restless and bristling.

Sean had been prevented from meeting with his musical colleagues "for clinical reasons." He was furious but managed to control himself: he could see that the staff were looking for any little sign. He got his violin, however, sans strings. At least it was safe with him. To survive he kept to himself and let the crazies do their thing. They were harmless enough. It surprised him to no end that the zenith of nursing care consisted of offering cigarettes and coffee. Just be good, he told himself, and then don't look back. Get away from the stench and the filth and the deranged troglodytic staff and don't look back. If this was a consequence of smoking weed, he'd be stone cold sober the rest of his life.

Then, finally, he got the word. Tomorrow he'd be out of the pit and onto the other side of the ward, where less dangerous patients were housed. Sean wasn't worried about patients.

'Will Joseph be transferred too?'

'That's none of your business, mate.'

Joseph, who claimed he was a past master of the guitar – 'All us Maoris play, bro!' – was fascinated by Sean's fiddle.

'I bet it sounds awesome.'

'Yeah,' Sean admitted, 'sometimes.'

Joseph took the violin in hand and inspected the purfling. He ran his fingers around the sides, back and belly and then along the unstrung fingerboard with earnest delicacy. He told Sean it reminded him of a Maori weapon.

A door was opened and Sean was about to be escorted into the promised land of the Open Side.

'Back off, Joe,' urged a small unkempt woman, ostensibly a nurse, but who knew?

Joseph did the eyebrow thing to Sean and whispered, 'Trust me, bro.' With Sean's violin in hand he began a kind of dance, showing impressive manipulation of the instrument while he chanted, widened his eyes and stuck out his tongue. Everyone froze. Sean's hair was curling at the sight.

Wielding the violin before him like a warrior, he charged through the unlocked door, offloaded the fiddle back to the bewildered musician and scampered out into a larger court-yard, where he leapt onto and over its roof to wherever freedom could be.

A week later as Sean left the Michael Fowler Centre with his colleagues a large muscular brown man approached.

'Joseph!'

They pressed noses and Joseph beckoned him to his car, a rusted number parked illegally nearby. He popped the trunk and extracted some kind of spear. It was stunning, with its smooth wooden blade, intricately carved face and tuft of feathers.

'It's a taiaha, bro. Me to you. Kia kaha.'

Violin Caprice No. 16

The beautiful, beautiful Beatrice – for there was no doubt about that rare exquisite beauty animated from some irrepressible Bacchic font within – where was I? Yes, her first true stroke of genius. She had given the Beethoven concerto in Vienna and the great city was in an uproar. The dazzling spectacle of her magnificent allure, palpably intoxicating, was matched only by an unflagging line of ravishing tone that flowed from her charged violin and into the capacious and majestic Musikverein.

A day later after such an incomparable triumph, she awoke to find her left hand flaccid and unresponsive. Instead of sinking into tears or submitting to panic, horror or self-pity, instead, mind you, of beginning a frantic medical odyssey leading to nowhere, she recognised the signs, paid homage to fate and turned the blow to her supreme advantage. Taking her agent into confidence immediately she informed him that on the day of the performance she had horribly sprained her fingers while breaking a fall (it was the accursed Viennese winter and the streets were treacherous) but chose not to disappoint the audience nor the composer she revered above all, and played through the injury, heedless of the consequences. Everywhere everyone was horrified by her calamity but unanimous in their unabashed reverence. She was hailed: Beethoven's Heroine, Vienna's Goddess of Music!

Concertgoers remembered now how at the beginning of the third movement she winced, how that comely face flashed anguish for the briefest of moments before serenely concealing its torment for their sake, and for Beethoven's! The more astute among them recalled the slight twitch of her bare left shoulder as she concluded, and others more trenchant now recollected the erratic heaving of her bosom: all, in retrospect, sure signs of her awful distress! Was ever such stoic bravery and self-sacrifice seen in the annals of performance? As she herself meekly reflected, 'Was Beethoven, was Vienna not worth it?' How the fractious press united in lionising her!

But I am getting ahead of myself.

Several days later her hand had fully recovered, and this is where the absolute genius of that woman revealed itself.

What may appear impulsive is generally the outward culmination of a long-held and deeply felt inner conviction, a conviction arrived at beneath the flow of superficial events and seeking only the right moment to be realised. In truth Beatrice had been tiring of the career. All fine musicians are arrant sensualists – of the ear. Some choose to confine their pleasure to that narrow canal. Beatrice could not be so constrained. Her Dionysian desire for the richest and most transcendent of sensual pleasures could be checked no longer and she chose to alter her circumstances so as to allow Eros full scope. At the age of thirty-five she counted on at least two decades of joyful indulgence. If the violin had already warranted thirty years, did not an exploration of human love require at least as much? Was she not already in arrears? Physical beauty, no matter how great, did not last forever.

I shake my head when I think of her stratagem and her vision. Within months she had received invitations, now that she was no longer playing, to adjudicate scores of musical competitions. And by the summer she was presiding, thanks to the boundless generosity of ardent admirers, principally ex-lovers, over festivals established under her aegis in Switzerland and the Rocky Mountains, festivals that attracted the best students and the most glittering masters, festivals imbued with her beguiling charm, festivals that grew in fame, festivals over which she commanded like a goddess, festivals where careers could be made, broken or wither, depending on her whim. Naturally she held a private studio as well, and the brightest aspirants sought her out.

Can you not see the brilliance? Liberated from the dull and implacable routine of technical practice, she could yet keep music-making at the centre, for it was an essential part of her soul – but only a part. By all accounts she was a mischievously delightful lover, but now she raised her talents to undreamed heights. The infinite subtleties of seduction, the varied nuances of tension and release – what after all was the art of music but the art of knowing how to seduce, how to create an ebb and flow of energies so as to captivate and transport?

Every worthy talent in that small but fascinating Valhalla of the elite swam into her ken and, if she chose, her bed. She was far from being a selfish lover: those on whom she showered her delights would never have known such pleasure. But she demanded much as well, and occasionally she, having inspired her consorts, received unanticipated rewards.

She developed a taste for youth, for the personality as yet not wholly formed and therefore giving the incomparable illusion of limitless possibility and adventure. The "sophisticated" lover held no interest any longer. No, it was the young she sought, the brilliant, boisterous, confident yearning untrammelled young, and they teemed round her by design.

She learned over time to read a universe in a caress, to take the imprint of a soul with a kiss, to inflame with the smallest of words or gestures, to elicit obsession, upheaval and ecstasy. She studied the effects of the minutest variations of breath and pressure and voice on her subjects, how, for example, the faintest darting flick of her tongue along the inner lobe of the ear, timed properly, could induce a swoon! The variations were endless, endless, and the instrument, the human body, so superior to the puny violin in its capacity to respond! Why, lives had been altered by the stroke of a fingertip, a word exhaled, a glance – lives that would alter others in turn. She proved a most profound scholar of the human spirit, having divined its sensual key.

The transience and variety of her liaisons merely heightened their value. Oh, occasionally something untoward might occur, an accident in the mountains, broken hearts leading to broken careers for the weak who craved permanence; but the air of risk and of danger only deepened her impossible allure. She had become a Helen, an Aphrodite – no, even greater: she had become the supreme artist of the supreme art.

And yet ...

It was in Switzerland that she met Sophie, a blossoming violinist, physically captivating of course, radiant and as insatiable in her pursuit of life's gifts as Beatrice was. They stalked each other for weeks in that Alpine heaven with its scent of pine, murmur of streams, wildflowers nestled midst towering forested heights and night-time concerts under a canopy of stars.

At master classes Beatrice purred to Sophie, or grazed her hand to demonstrate a technical matter on the bow. Sophie would smile with moist lips, feign naïveté, arch her neck in a way that made it impossible not to wish to cover it with kisses, or reveal a glimpse of her own indomitable fire. Beatrice was bewitched. The young cellist whom she was cultivating and had recently enjoyed was instantly forgotten and ignored, despite his urgent and bewildered entreaties.

In Sophie's absence the hours grew unendurably long, so Beatrice found a way to her rehearsals as if by chance. At first they were a delight but as Beatrice's desire grew, they became a source of torment. She read in every glance Sophie bestowed on a colleague something that made her uneasy. She took her blushes as rejection and her thanks as disdain. Although still incomparably beautiful herself she began to envy Sophie her younger animal grace and vigour.

The novelty of these tumultuous feelings held its own charm for a while but the intensity of their hold frightened her. One day Sophie casually requested some particular help on a passage in Saint-Saen's *Havanaise*. At her cottage that memorable evening Beatrice was taught a lesson.

In truth both were smitten, both fearful, both consumed, but youth was on Sophie's side, with its avenue of years ahead. Beatrice pulled every string to launch her career and the young virtuoso dazzled as she herself once did. Their travels allowed them to rendezvous and sustain each other's explorations but whereas Beatrice had lost all interest in others, Sophie was still susceptible to the numerous temptations that came with her ascent in that small but ever so concentrated and flattering world.

Rumours eventually reached Beatrice that her lover had met an Italian nobleman and was engaged. Not only was the man wealthy and cultured, she learned, but he was also alleged to be intelligent and, worst and most threatening of all, a genuine poet.

Sophie, clearly infatuated, had begun to grow distant. Her calls were fewer, her protestations of love infrequent, the demands of her concert schedule ever more imposing. Beatrice lost weight, flew into unprovoked rages, cancelled lessons and engagements without notice and neglected auditions for her festivals. She thought only of Sophie's long red hair, full sweet lips and golden eyes, eyes in which she saw the unattainable and unfathomable dream of life itself.

Learning of Sophie's recital in, of all places, Vienna, Beatrice pleaded and Sophie surrendered, agreeing to meet, but only briefly and in secrecy, fearing to disturb the delicate balance of relations with a fiancé she strove to convince herself she loved.

Beatrice arrived at the Hotel Bristol on the eve of her performance. She had done everything in her power to enhance her beauty and the effect was not lost upon the violinist. Sophie's heart raced and despite herself she yearned to reach out to the older woman in a wild embrace.

'I've come to make amends to my girl with golden eyes,' cooed Beatrice, cradling Sophie's face before their kiss, 'to give, not to receive.'

And give she did. Beatrice purposefully remained clothed as she ravished the younger woman and with tenderness, teasing and ferocity, with every art in her arsenal, drew screams from Sophie that caused snickers in the hotel corridors, screams that left her hoarse. Sophie pleaded, despite exhaustion, to give in return, but Beatrice adamantly refused.

Instead, she took the gloriously spent woman's left hand and kissed her fingers with utmost delicacy. She kissed them and then, in one deft motion, bent and twisted the ring finger sideways at the joint above the knuckle, before slipping silently away.

The stunned Sophie screamed again, but voicelessly, and although she had the presence of mind to pop the digit back into its socket, it throbbed with pain and began to swell conspicuously before her tear-filled golden eyes.

If you recall I made mention of Beatrice's first stroke of genius. This was the second. You see, anything more violent – more *gauche* – would never have done: no, it was the perfect solution.

You may perhaps have been wondering how I myself could be privy to all that I describe, yes, and rightly so. Well, almost immediately Sophie told me that she had been accosted by a jealous and bitter rival who, no longer able to perform, bore her ill for her success, leaving out what was most pertinent, namely, the nature of the accosting and the history of their passion. She wished to call the police but I recommended against it: in Italy the police are the last to be involved; in fact, they are treacherous and useless. No, we Italians knew how to manage such matters. Leave it to me.

I armed myself and tracked the witch down. It was child's play – she would only be staying in one of a handful of hotels. At the Sacher my subtle inquiries achieved success: after ascertaining her room number, I purloined several towels from the laundry. Concealing my vengeful intent under the guise of subservience, I knocked and held the towels before me as if casually replenishing a guest's necessaries.

She opened the door to her suite and there she stood. You must remember that within the hour this magnificent woman had been in the throes of love, but herself had not been satisfied. She exuded before me furious extravagant desire. Tall, with smouldering dark eyes and dark flowing tresses, her bosom beckoning, her every limb poised ...

'I was expecting you,' she said. 'What took you so long?'

The towels tumbled from my arms. That evening I passed the most glorious hours of my life, sensible of transcendence as only a poet can be.

Oh, I should mention that Sophie, poor thing, eventually joined an orchestra, consorting with the likes of conductors, of all people. A pity.

Violin Caprice No. 17

Every year, when the circus came to his little village, Dr. Menard sang in his heart. He admonished his patients not to fall ill during the week of festivity, and to encourage them in their health he dispensed his services with even more than his usual generosity. The villagers, lest they arouse the effulgent anger of their good doctor, took great care of themselves; of course they too wanted to be in the best of conditions to experience the joys of the itinerant entertainers.

Menard's wife, a modest and devoted woman, was glad to see her husband relieved of his daily rounds. During the circus he tended only to emergencies, and these were generally dispatched with the application of a cold compress to the forehead and a stern warning about the dangers of excessive drink. The additional time together at home was a joy seldom allowed, and they took full advantage of it. Their unhurried talk over morning coffee burst with the year's unexpressed sweetness.

Towards noon Madame Menard could see the rising excitement of anticipation in the eyes of her husband as he sent messages inviting several of the poorest children to be his guests. It was an honour to be among those chosen to sit with the imposing but jovial doctor at the performances – so much so that the village rich often pleaded with the doctor to confer much-needed esteem upon their offspring and thus add to the glory of their progenitors. That they would suffer their sons and daughters to sit with the impoverished and deprived was a measure of Menard's inestimable prestige. But, honest man that he was, he held steadfast in the face of provincial flattery.

On the first day of the circus, held in the open air on a serenely beautiful afternoon, the late summer's light having lost its harshness, Menard relished the merriment of his companions as they watched the jugglers, clowns, and tumblers. The jokes were not especially funny, nor were the acrobatics breathtaking, but the liberated gaiety of the villagers transformed the mediocre troupe into consummate artists.

When the time came for the customary trapeze and high-wire acts, which seldom varied from year to year, the crowd was prepared to be thrilled. They gaped with awe as the muscular men and women twirled in the air after leaping from such slender bars, and marvelled at the strength of their grasp. True, were an accident to happen no great damage could be done, for a sturdy net protected them from any serious consequence of miscues; but the villagers gasped nonetheless, and when the first artist fell they rose en masse in alarm.

Here Menard gladly assumed his physicianly responsibilities and rushed to the floor to pronounce the embarrassed acrobat unharmed. The villagers applauded and the doctor himself reddened with pride as the circus troupe bowed and blew kisses his way.

For Menard the day could not have been more perfect. As he settled in for the last event he let his mind wander to the days of his youth, which had been marked more by curiosity than by passion. He awoke from his brief reverie when the urchin by his side cried out at the removal of the net for the high-wire walker. This was extraordinary indeed! The doctor could remember nothing like this in all the years of his circus-going, and was on the verge of protesting in the sober name of Medicine when the artist appeared.

She stood on a small platform atop a pole some twenty-five feet from the ground. Her face was plain, but her torso was wonderfully appealing. Her legs showed muscles seen mainly in the textbooks of anatomy.

Menard gazed at the lithe form, quite transfixed, as it journeyed with utter confidence from pole to pole across the taut slender cord. Whether her arms were outstretched, above her head or by her side, whether she took small or large steps, she gave the picture of unerring balance.

The doctor's eye, so used to ferret out the subtle messages of discomfort, could discern nothing but beauteous disdain for imperfection.

Later that night, at the café to which the troupe repaired, Menard spied the girl as she revelled with her companions. Her long black hair hung in a braid and her eyes sparkled. Just then a member of the circus took it in his head to order a glass of sherry for the kind doctor, which he acknowledged with aplomb. He was, after all, on familiar ground, and had known and treated the owners of the café for years. He alone of the villagers was permitted to remain while the circus members ate and drank, ostensibly in his unofficial function of attendant physician.

The villagers had learned long ago that privacy was the best policy when it came to travelling entertainers, and that night-time minglings inevitably led to menacing disruptions of both circus and village life. So they reined and nursed their yearnings, preserving their release only for the sanctioned realm of the performances.

Menard greeted and lauded the performers in his gen-
tlemanly way. He heard with an attentive ear the accounts
of illness, suggested various remedies, promised to bring
unguents and powders, and dispensed important advice
about the prevention of disease.

His heart leapt when he unexpectedly came face to face
with the high-wire artist. She smiled and thanked him for so
quickly coming to the aid of her colleague earlier in the day.
He blushed this time with the pleasure of having caught her
attention and furtively kept an eye out for the girl's consort.
To his surprise and disturbing delight, however, one did not
appear. Though friendly and easy with all, she was romanti-
cally unattached: this Menard could infer easily enough, for
the stigmata of passion tend to be clearer to those unmarked.

While she danced playfully with her companions, he
slowly sipped his drink and smiled. His benevolent face
attracted her, and when a partner spun her across the floor
she settled at the doctor's table, a bit out of breath, and radiant. Menard called for a glass of wine which the girl accepted.
On such a night, cloudless and cool, Menard could not help
but gush.

'May I say, my dear woman, that you were extraordinary
today? The epitome of balance! I salute you, I drink to you,
an artist of the highest calibre!'

'I think you go too far, doctor. What you call balance
is something for which I strive continually, but have never
achieved.'

'What? Understand, my friend – do you mind if I call you
such? – that I observed you, I and all the others, and what we
saw was perfection.'

'What is your name?' the artist abruptly inquired.

'Pierre,' replied the physician, simply, astonished at such familiarity.

'I will call you by your Christian name, since you have already deemed me a friend. My own is Jessica. By the way,' she added gratuitously, 'I have no need for a strongman, I rely on myself.'

The doctor was speechless, fearful of the twinge of lust that threatened to spoil the encounter. Jessica continued: 'I strive and fail to achieve the balance you say you cherish so much, that is my work. I suppose I am an illusionist then, since others fall in love with what I know to be false. But tell me of yours. You must be privy to so many secrets of the body.'

By this time Menard had recovered and began to brim with volubility, unaccustomed as he was to drink.

'Jessica, listen, my friend. I too seek balance, but fail miserably. My eye is keen for any perturbation of the natural harmony of the soul, which expresses itself through its host, the body. I am a detective, perhaps too good at discerning such maladies; and I minister to the body to restore matters. But even when successful, as in setting a bone, or ridding a wound of infection, I know I have not reached the source of disease, which resides – which can *only* reside – in the hearts of my patients.'

Menard checked himself, but Jessica seemed enchanted, so he was emboldened to go on.

'My dear Jessica, you may be too young to see that these ailments and accidents are caused from within. The role of external forces has been much overestimated.'

'So we are both failures,' said Jessica, prompting the two of them to laugh.

'No,' said the doctor, 'you do not see yourself as I do, as you *should* see yourself! Do you know, when I have time away from my practice, I search the animal kingdom for examples of the harmony and balance you so miraculously have attained, in the hope of divining their secrets and bequeathing them to my fellow men. I wish I could show you!'

Jessica rose suddenly and extended her hand. 'I would be honoured.'

Menard took without hesitation the artist's small hand in his own, and the two of them slipped quietly away unobserved. They moved silently along a narrow country road to a small hut where the doctor kept his collections, a resting place on his rounds. The uppermost leaves of the trees swayed and rustled and the stars seemed palpably near.

With gentle gallantry he held the door for Jessica. Hastily he lit a small fire, and then led her round to his specimens, chosen for their brilliant symmetries. Jessica was attentive, and cradled the plants and insects with care while the doctor described their beauties. Then, strangely, for he had not intended it, he began to complain about time, its shortage, the pressures of his routine, the prevention of his research, the brevity of life even. Jessica spied a small violin case tucked away in a shelf, and inquired. With his tacit permission she opened it and beheld a miniature but still pristine instrument. She ran her hand over its curiously taut strings, each in tune, and surmised. Menard shrugged.

Jessica unbraided her hair and let it fall freely behind her. It hung, dark and lustrously, far below her waist. With a quick gesture she flung her head forward and spun and parted her hair into two thick strands, which she held at either side.

'I think, dear doctor,' she whispered, 'that you may be looking in the wrong places for your ineffable harmony.'

Pierre gazed steadily at Jessica and placed his hands gingerly upon her waist. The delicious scent of the surrounding fields and the aroma rising from the artist's breasts commingled to intoxicate. Jessica very slowly lifted her arms and coiled the soft strands of her hair around Pierre's neck, pulling his lips firmly to her own.

The lovers met nightly, ecstatically. Pierre had no need of words to describe the glow from within that began to radiate over every aspect of his life. His friends, his patients, his wife – he seemed to savour their idiosyncratic irregularities and saw their evils and goodnesses as never before. Could he leave the people and work he held so dear?

He continued to attend the circus and through the week was transported to see his lover negotiate her dangerous mission. He thought better of pleading with her to use the net, so he suffered greatly during her act – not through a lack of confidence in her abilities, but a selfish disbelief in his own good fortune. However, such suffering was not without rewards, for each evening their tensions would be blissfully explored and assuaged.

On their last night together Jessica and Pierre gave themselves to each other with exquisitely tender fire. Morning sunlight strengthened their embrace and caresses lingered perilously long. They kissed and kissed again and promised to make no promises for the future.

That day Pierre decided to attend the final performance on his own. He entered well after the show had begun and found an inconspicuous seat at the back. When Jessica made her entrance he nearly burst into tears and hid his face in his hands. But his lover spied him, and it was impossible to resist her gaze.

The audience quieted and Jessica began her approach, which the doctor could observe with incipient fear was very different. Had she lost her graces and strength somehow, had she become unnerved or desperate at their impending break? Would she plummet? He rose breathlessly to his feet.

The acrobat strolled across the tightrope as casually as one would saunter across a road, arms swinging lightly and naturally in rhythm with her gait. There were no artistic gestures, no arabesques. She turned and walked back from the second platform just as effortlessly, then bowed to the quiet and perplexed crowd before hurrying away and stealing a final glance at her beloved's astonished and happy mien.

Jessica never returned to the village. Many years later, when Pierre was readying himself for departure from the life that had given him much, and to which he had given much in turn, a strapping young stranger paid a visit. Rumour has it that not even the undertaker could alter the smile that transfixed the doctor's face.

Violin Caprice No. 18

Revenge is very much maligned. The maxims that caution one to avoid seeking it, the promotion of benevolence in the face of outright hostility, the encouragement to forget a grievance that has cut, which of course is utterly impossible – these are all signs of a weaker, less creative stratum of society, one that has been manipulated by its superiors who, though perhaps not experts themselves in revenge, are certainly masters in the trammelling and marauding of their underlings. They in fact make it a business to pre-empt the need for revenge.

Maestro Heinrich Seltzerlust was many things, but he was not meek. True, for the sake of his career he had agreed to the annual Event, but compromise, if he were to achieve his aspirations, was sadly essential. And at first it seemed a small price to pay for the opportunities to bring to the world the music that generally went unheard. Being a man who regarded melody as appeasement and economy as the apex of musical expression, believing for example that Cage's *4'33"* was too long by four minutes, it was of course enough of a trial to programme the tired Old Masters.

But here he was wise, for by insisting from the rabble he conducted on the utmost skill in executing such works, the obsolescence and the hypocrisy of "harmony unfurled" as Scriabin quaintly put it, would be exposed in its nakedness.

Whether the ignorant subscribers appreciated it consciously was another matter, but at least it gave him the opportunity to enlighten their souls with Stockhausen several times a year, deviously sandwiched between the chestnuts and war-horses.

Nonetheless, there was still the Board and particularly the two scions of the Board, the Hummels, octogenarian husband and wife, escort service entrepreneurs in their youth who made their fortune in cable television, and who had stipulated the Event upon his hiring; who were the source of the ensemble's funds, feeding its coffers; and who had veto power over every major decision. Even their reluctantly sponsored tour to Tahiti (where incidentally the native population showed a tremendous exuberance for serialism, thus demonstrating something about the hollowness of so-called civilising influences), could not counterbalance the Event, which had become insufferable.

Seltzerlust was not intrinsically an unkind man. Of course like any of his colleagues he would have sold his grandmother into slavery should it have been necessary to assume a post, but he drew the line at selling his soul. However, no matter how he pressed or inveigled to extricate himself from the loathsome obligatory performance Mr. and Mrs. Hummel would not budge.

The Event in and of itself seemed harmless: a children's concert on a lavish scale featuring the usual cutesy shenanigans, orchestral players in slapdash costume, hordes of uninterested brats, ages five through eleven, compelled to attend on pain of cell-phone deprivation and who infected the hall with that peculiar odour of unwashed feet, and the like. It was not even so much the clown suit that he, Maestro Heinrich Seltzerlust of Schleswig-Holstein was directed to wear.

No, these travails he could bear. What however for him was constitutionally unacceptable was the presence of the Hummel dog, a lethargic Doberman that was paraded into its cushioned seat at the commencement of the "fun" with its makeshift crown, and who alternately snoozed and growled during the length of the charade. To play for a dog, to play for the dog "King," to play for the dog "King" and the Hummels one more time was to forfeit his soul. Seltzerlust hated the dog and he hated the Hummels and he hated the Hummel Pavilion for the Performing Arts and he vowed revenge.

Germans, it should be noted, do not have the deserved reputation of the Italians for vengeance. Yes, for sadism they are unequalled, but vengeance requires subtlety. Seltzerlust was the exception: he knew his mind to be of the subtlest, and with a conviction buttressed by wielding the baton for the New Complexity, the New Simplicity and Post-Post-Minimalism, he devised a plan.

The Hummels were surprised and ecstatic when the Maestro, well in advance of the Event, evinced an unaccustomed enthusiasm and in the spirit of appealing widely to the masses, not to mention their own musical tastes, offered to have his son, an accomplished thirteen year old violinist – who like his father on the podium would also be accoutred in clown suit, and wasn't that the common touch! – play a medley of popular themes from the songbook of Sir Elton John.

'Dad,' said his son, snickering, 'are you sure about this?'

'Perfectly.'

'And you'll get me the uncensored *Grand Theft Auto*?'

He had bargained hard and the Maestro had no choice but to relent.

'Yes,' he coughed.

'Okay, I'm in.' Bartleby's angelic face masked a very active lurking devil within. He saw his father in a new and most impressive light.

On the day of the Event Seltzerlust was buoyant, daring even to whistle a snatch from Berg. His lawyer was in attendance, as were several members of the Fourth Estate. In a way, he thought, it was all so simple, too simple even – could he not prolong the crescendo, the more to savour his triumph?

He marched to the podium and turning his clown-bedecked head with its orange bouffant wig and bulbous red nose to the aged Hummels and their unsuspecting beast, he smiled. King snarled and the Hummels shooshed him with unadulterated cloying indulgence. All the better.

The masses hummed and buzzed, occasionally chuckling at the puerile antics onstage. Why do horn players enjoy debasing themselves by mimicking the sounds of digestion? An American thing, no doubt.

The programme unfolded until at last it was time for the younger Seltzerlust to emerge with his violin. He moved gingerly and slowly, looking a bit unwieldy in his large billowy costume, but looking like a clown, which was the point after all. The so-called music of Sir Elton John was his greatest challenge, for it acted upon him like ipecac, but he soldiered on.

King awoke from his doze when the scent of a freshly cut slab of steak wafted his way. And after the elder Seltzerlust surreptitiously blew his trusty Galton whistle it was the work of a millisecond for the Doberman to bound out of his cushioned throne and onto the stage, tearing into the seat of Bartleby's costume trousers, where the meat had been expertly hidden. The boy yelled as instructed, his father declaimed, 'He's killing my son!' and the entire hall erupted into pandemonium. The Hummels turned spectrally pale at the reflexively instantaneous worry of legal action.

When both parties and their lawyers met to negotiate a deal to prevent a public suit, Seltzerlust's salary was tripled, the Event cancelled, a trust fund established for his son's anticipated Post-Traumatic Stress Disorder treatment, and after a fiercely waged battle, Stockhausen's *Licht* given the go-ahead for next season.

'*Leaked*?' said Mrs. Hummel.

'I think he said *Licked*,' replied her husband.

'A musical?'

'Something like that.' He winked at his wife.

'Hold on there, Maestro,' boomed Mr. Hummel. 'I have an even better idea.'

Seltzerlust was regally curious.

'Why not a whole season of your man? Go ahead, go for it. We're behind you.'

Seltzerlust could hardly believe his ears.

'Yeah, you heard me. You're the genius, that's why we hired you in the first place.'

* * *

Seltzerlust pried Bartleby away from the unspeakable mayhem he coordinated on the gargantuan plasma screen and gave him the news. It should be mentioned that wearing ice hockey pants under his capacious clown suit had been a complete success.

'Sounds good, dad, except maybe that's a little too much Stockhausen.'

'How can there be too much Stockhausen?'

Well, after a year Seltzerlust found out. Losing most of his audience and many of his musicians did not exactly work to his advantage and when his contract was due for renewal the Board had no choice but to allow him to seek opportunities elsewhere, opportunities being very very few for so highly specialised a conductor.

Naturally Seltzerlust again craved revenge, an even greater and more exacting kind, and vengeful fantasies consumed him. That was bad enough. But the indelible link that had been forged between the idea of vengeance and the tunes of Sir Elton John ... One can scarcely imagine the poor soul's torment. This not even the Hummels had anticipated.

Violin Caprice No. 19

We gazed out over the lazy harbour on a cool Spring evening. The darkening blue film of the sea's surface shimmered like a silky skin begging to be peeled away.

My friend Donato, with whom I often shared a cup, sat listlessly. As a musician fighting the good fight with his modest fiddle against the relentless and overwhelming assaults of popular culture he often lapsed into a self-protective reverie when the batteries fired again, as they did now with the thirteenth replay of "Ebony and Ivory" at an adjacent Lido café.

'Shall we?' I asked, ready to adjourn elsewhere.

He shrugged, opened his eyes and merely twitched a corner of his mouth as if to say 'What use? There is no escape.' The ever-moving ever-sibilant sea was consolation, so we remained where we were. I was content enough to continue our discussion once he re-emerged.

'Marcello,' he grumbled at length, the Englishman knew us better than we know ourselves. 'A lust of the blood and a permission of the will: the essence of Venetian love.'

'Don't be so cynical, my friend. The author of *Othello*, whoever he was, cannot be confined to the viewpoint of his greatest villain. His vast tapestry depicts human – and even Venetian – love in the multitude of its manifestations. But there was one facet of which even he, the greatest psychologist of all, surpassing our beloved Dante, was ignorant.'

Donato pricked his ears.

'What, another never to be published poem of yours in which you have divined a profound truth?'

'Greater than a poem, Donato: a method, a method that being foolproof even you yourself may employ, that is if you regard the seduction of women to be a worthy goal.'

'My violin is proof enough of my powers,' he replied.

'For an ever-diminishing coterie, perhaps.' The nauseating song was being repeated yet again, to the delight of the bovine crowd. Perhaps I was being a bit mischievous: I knew that Donato had recently been spurned by a woman who, in his opinion, had no right, no matter how married she may have been.

'Go ahead, Marcello, amuse me.'

I called for coffees – that stimulating beverage always fortifies – and began my discourse. I told Donato how, though hardly a rival to the great ancient and modern authors in literary achievement, I had been granted, through the agency of a dream, a most remarkable – and practical – insight. In a spirit of generosity and in celebration of our friendship, I would share it with him and him alone whilst I laboured to mould it into poetic shape. In fact, I added, should he choose to test my hypothesis, I would be not only honoured but grateful, for his triumphs would serve as icing on the cake.

'Not another Calabrian get-rich-quick scheme, I hope.'

'No, perhaps not quick, and as far as riches go, it depends how one defines them.'

'Don't be such a tease – out with it!'

'Donato,' I said, 'I have discovered the secret of seduction. None but the most primitive of women, and they would hardly be worth seducing anyway, will be able to resist. But first, tell me the kind of woman who appeals to you.'

'As if you don't know! Well, I'll indulge you. She must be physically appealing, not necessarily in conventional ways, and certainly not of the anorexic type promulgated by our worthless mass media. No, there must be something about her look that captivates. And because I pride myself on *not* being a connoisseur who is, after all, only an expert of exclusion, I can appreciate the greater scope of beauty. Not unlike Don Giovanni.'

We both laughed: he had revealed his hero.

'But the physical is hardly enough,' he continued seriously. 'A woman worthy of desire must love something beyond herself. And here too I am not fussy. It can be anything so long as she has not been enslaved to the tripe we cannot avoid hearing in our public places.'

'By anything you mean ... ?'

'Anything – scientific, artistic, social, political, geological, environmental, meteorological, marine ... '

'Yes, yes, I get the picture,' I responded, cutting him off. 'Now, let's say you find a woman who intrigues you. You wish to engage her attention, you wish to incite her passion, you wish her to fall so rapturously and richly in love with you that your all-encompassing encounters will transport. Am I correct?'

'You mean, and pardon me for translating your poetry, Marcello, that I wish to have a wonderful time in bed?'

'Go ahead, be crass about it.' We laughed again, and I proceeded. 'After you have met your target you will have discovered that she has a quest. Is there someone you have in mind?'

'As a matter of fact, there is. Not the impervious degenerate who rebuffed me, by the way, but someone I've only recently met. Cassandra.'

'Good, now tell me a little about her.'

'Aside from the fact that she is ravishingly beautiful, with naturally blonde hair cut to perfection to frame the noble and intelligent features of her sensual face, enchanting blue eyes, skin as smooth as our ocean's ... '

'Yes, yes, all that is given, but what else?'

'Oh, she is an aspiring novelist.'

Now we were getting somewhere. You see, Donato has a way of losing himself, a typical fiddler of course.

'And what exactly does she aspire to write about?'

'The *Mona Lisa*.'

'The *Mona Lisa*?'

'Yes, it's brilliant.'

'Of course the *Mona Lisa* is brilliant.'

'No, her idea, the projected novel.'

I had my doubts, but I encouraged him to elaborate.

'She wishes to write a romantic novel about Leonardo's affair with Lisa Gherardini, *La Gioconda* herself, an affair that led to his tutoring her in the art of painting, which then enabled her to depict herself, which posterity mistakenly believes is the handiwork of Leonardo.'

'Hmmm ... yes, well, the actual content is not so important for my methodology. But she's perfect.'

'She certainly is,' he added dreamily.

'Perfect as a test case,' I interjected.

'Her husband can be a nuisance.'

'Husbands often are. When will you talk to her again?'

'In a fortnight. She is one of our donors and under the pretext of establishing the new programme for next year, I invited her to a café.'

'And what is your plan of attack?'

'Very simple. After a discussion of the musical selections she is inclined to favour, I would speak to her of her beauty, of its effect, of her eyes, her lips, of how I have been moved to greater artistry, of how I vainly attempt to express such beauties on my violin, etc. Mostly true. The usual.'

I was beginning to suspect that Donato would have been attracted to a Cassandra without aspirations, but he reassured me to the contrary.

'My dear friend,' I replied, not without condescension, 'you are going about it all wrong! No wonder your track record is so dismal. Now, listen, forget that nonsense. Even if it works it works for the wrong reasons.'

'When you meet her,' I urged, 'you must resist the obvious, you must betray no attraction to anything, and I mean anything *except*' – and this I emphasised as strongly as possible – '*except her novel writing*. Fasten onto it like a terrier onto a rat. Evince fascination, encouragement, speak of other novels and yet the importance of the new voice in the novel, tell her about how you have tried your hand but failed – and this too is important, that you have failed – but above all, show reverence for novelists and incredible awe for her literary pursuits.'

I also advised him to dress down for the occasion: he was under no circumstances whatsoever to give the impression of attempting to woo.

'If you must use saltpetre before you see her, so be it!' I declared in conclusion.

Donato seemed to be intrigued, though he questioned me on certain points.

'But what if she is already charmed and interested? Isn't your method superfluous?'

Poor fellow, to be so shallow.

'Donato, this is seduction on a higher plane, not your common garden variety, the kind that flowers briefly and then rots. This is seduction that will endure and sustain you. Your method is hit and miss: trust me, this is sure-fire.'

Not even "Ebony and Ivory" could break our spell as we contemplated action. Sipping the dregs of my fourth demi-tasse, I leaned forward and placed a hand on my friend's shoulder. 'This is about the psychology of women, which as a poet has been my life's work.'

Just over a fortnight later a beaming Donato accosted me with such hearty surprise that I lost the lion's share of a particularly well-brewed espresso on my latest sartorial acquisition, a cream-coloured linen-and-silk blazer.

'Don't worry, I'll pay for the cleaning bill!' he exclaimed.

He could hardly contain himself as he described his rendezvous with Cassandra.

'You know, I was even tempted to bring flowers,' he began to my horror, 'but I trusted you, and trust has never been so well placed.'

He described in great detail how he had checked his natural impulses and focussed on Cassandra's book and ideas. He reported how – and here he, being a musician and therefore clumsy with words had to grope for a while – how he was positively "metaphysical," the upshot of which was that it had all worked like a charm. A soft gleaming of Cassandra's eyes confirmed everything, and he had to quell the joyful dance within his breast to preserve a stoically intellectual exterior. She had even proposed meeting several days later – to discuss the musical programming further, ha! – but he demurred, and on hearing this I was duly impressed.

'You have potential, Donato! Now, the second critical aspect of the methodology, and this is indeed critical, my friend, is patience. Patience, patience, patience. Do you get me?'

'Patience ... but for how long?'

'For however long is necessary.'

'But how long is that? I can barely control myself as it is.'

The weaknesses of the man were writ large. I overcame the impulse to shake him by his cheap lapels.

'Stick to the *Mona Lisa* and novels, and when she reaches boiling point come and see me again – but no sooner than a month!'

Thirty-one days later Donato was at my door with a three hundred euro bottle of champagne.

'You are worth far far more my dear Marcello!' he exclaimed, embracing me. I invited him into my home and we toasted the impending consummation, but he still required some sage guidance.

'Remember,' I cautioned, 'accept her caresses, her desire, her everything tonight, but praise only her book, her ideas. I repeat: none of the usual claptrap about her breasts or hair or eyes!'

Scarcely another month had gone by when Donato personally delivered a *case* of the very same expensive champagne.

I was delighted, for at long last, despite whatever shortcomings I may have had as a contemporary poet, the acuteness of my observation had proved my rank with the masters. I asked Donato about his violin.

'What violin?'

'Your violin, your music.'

'What about it?'

'Never mind.'

After three months however it was a frantic and dishevelled Donato who burst upon me one evening at my home.

'You and your damned novel!'

'You mean Cassandra's novel.'

'You know what I mean!' he shouted.

'Donato, calm down, what's wrong? Has she rejected you? Did you diverge from the method?'

'Diverge? Are you kidding me? No, like an utter fool I stayed true! I followed your infernal advice to the letter. And now? And now? And now?'

'And now?'

'And now she's confessed to her husband that she's found her true love, that she is filing for divorce and that she is devoted to me and to me alone.'

I could see the tragedy.

'If that brute of a husband doesn't kill me.'

'He won't.'

'How do you know?'

'You told me he was an accountant.'

'True. Well, even if I survive, I don't want to be imprisoned. I wanted something very simple, just a magnificent, passionate, engulfing, marvelous – but *contained* thing. Something to add a jaunt to the step, spice to my music. Speaking of which, she is now forever pressing me about the violin, my repertoire, my interpretative "stance" as she puts it.'

'No, the same method does not work to seduce men. In fact, it is a repellent.'

'Marcello,' he whimpered, 'I wanted something manageable and this woman, beautiful as she may be, this Cassandra – she wants love! I think it may even be worse: she may also want marriage. I need your help. Please, use your poetic psychology in reverse, whatever, and get me out of this mess. I need to get rid of her!'

'Have you thought of telling her you don't love her?'

'Of course, *cretino*, but she doesn't believe me! *A man, she says, who doesn't love me would hardly commune with my aspirations as you have. Don't try to spare me the hardships of divorce and true love, Donato, love which your sensitive and self-effacing soul cannot disguise.*'

'Let's open a bottle. It will help me to think.'

After the second magnum of even the most superb champagne, superbness becomes intrinsically less evident than simple alcohol content. We might have been drinking Asti Spumante for all it mattered. Donato slept over for the night and I on awakening in the wee hours made coffee. For sheer creative punch the combination of coffee and a poetic mind cannot be surpassed. Suffice it to say, I had come up with a plan.

Several days later in one of Venice's out of the way treasures of a café I made the acquaintance of this notorious Cassandra, Marcello having arranged for us to meet as I had directed. If anything, my friend had underestimated her allure. The ecstatic anguish of love had given her features a depth that could easily inspire a few hundred scattered rhymes.

I told her the truth – well, the most important part of it, and she, poor woman, broke down, though with quiet dignity. To a meridionale like myself natural blonde hair of such softness and eyes of such ocean-like blue were as striking as the quiet spasms of her snowy bosom.

'So he really had no interest in my book?' she inquired tearfully.

'I'm afraid not,' I sighed. 'But,' I added spontaneously, having taken pity at the sight of this great and beautiful woman, this woman who was prepared to sacrifice marriage and material prosperity for a fiddler, 'I personally thought the idea was pure genius. Donato is a musician, not a man of words. We poets perceive things differently.'

Donato went back to his old ways, captivating with his fiddle the few who would listen and flitting from one fleeting admirer to the next as he excoriated the world of pervasively poor taste.

I on the other hand, well, I decided to give poetry a bit of a break and stretch myself out in another form.

After our potboiler hit the supermarket stands the biggest challenge Cassandra and I faced was how to minimise taxes. Fortunately her ex wasn't a man to hold a grudge. Nor was Donato, who cheerfully played at our wedding, though he sneaked in a version of that dreadful song just as we cut the cake!

Violin Caprice No. 20

Brutus would not have accused my father of ambition. Nor would my mother, who spent a lot of time resting in bed while my dad smoked cigars and listened to the Quintet of the Hot Club of France, especially after one of their arguments, arguments that always seemed to be about ambition, or lack of.

'Are you going to be a mailman all your life?' Mom didn't so much as ask a question but make a bitter and resigned accusation.

'What do you have against the U.S. Postal Service?' Dad replied.

That's when she went upstairs slamming as many doors as possible on her way. Then came the sweet acrid smoke of Dad's cigar, which I could smell from my bedroom, followed by the gypsy guitar of Django Reinhardt and the wild violin of Stephane Grappelli, which I could hear.

My friend Olivia Cingolini plays violin: not at all like Grappelli. I'm not sure exactly how she plays but when I saw her at Assembly with her high school orchestra she looked so different from the gawky tomboy I grew up with and, like my friends, never gave a lustful thought about. Her sister, just two years older was already going out with college kids, for obvious reasons. But Chink – that was her nickname – is about as curvy as a cyclone fence and so shy you'd think she wanted her face to turn inside out. Onstage, however, with her violin she positively glowed into a new girl and when she smiled she seemed awfully cute, though it looks like I'm in the minority of one because my friends think she's still a dog, with or without the violin. What do they know, anyway?

Cingolini was enough of a reason to call her Chink, but there was more to it than that. In grade school she was the only girl allowed to play chink with us boys during recess, and if you don't know anything about the game let me explain. All you need is a wall and a pimple ball and a bunch of kids. The object is to hit the ball on a bounce against the wall so that the person following you can't do the same. If you smash it right into the crack between the wall and pavement, that's "chink." It's a game of angles and Chink was especially good at the soft shot that skimmed the wall obliquely and left no bounce for the next person to pick up. She often beat the crap out of us.

The other reasons for the name were that she had slightly slanty eyes, most unusual for an Italian girl, but then again her mother was Irish, so I guess you could expect anything from intermarriage. Plus she played the violin, and the only girls we Italian kids knew who played the violin were chinks, you know, Asians, whom I call Asians and not chinks, just to make things clear.

Chink and I were in our first year at Central and Girls High, single-sex public high schools for smart kids situated right next to each other and a long subway ride away from the neighbourhood. I worked up the guts to say something about the orchestra when I had my freshman baseball uniform on after a game while we were riding home. She seemed surprised, since I had hardly spoken to her except to cut her up in a friendly kind of way when we used to play chink, even though we have a lot in common: we're both self-conscious to the point of morbidity and we both get picked on by our friends for our looks and lack of athletic grace, despite being good at chink, which however isn't a real sport.

'So you play violin?' I ventured as the subway car swayed.

'So you play baseball?' she retorted.

Good one.

Now, about me and baseball. I made the team because I could pitch in the strike zone when I tried out. When I pitch for the team in an actual game I generally have one great inning, striking out the opposing side who are initially fooled by my big wind-up into thinking I can throw heat. Once they wise up they rip my one-speed slow ball to shreds. Which brings me back to my dad.

Maybe he lacked ambition but he didn't lack for making me feel that whatever I did was pretty okay. So at baseball practice, where he was the only father in the stands because as a postman his shift ended earlier than working hours for other dads, he applauded everything I did, and loudly. It was downright embarrassing. One day I surrendered nine runs in a single inning and when I slunk off the field he gave me an "attaboy champ" as if I had pitched a shutout. I guess I loved him for that little thing, and for showing me how to throw a curveball, and for kissing me on the cheek without making me feel it was funny – which was the Italian in him. He knew I was a runt and had trouble with the neighbourhood kids, but he let me work it out on my own. Once I was getting the hell beaten out of me by a jerk and my father rushed out of the house onto the street. Instead of grabbing the kid and pushing him away from me he simply folded his arms and watched. I fought back as hard as I could but was no match for the bully. Every time he hit me I went at him for more, never landing so much as a single punch. He left only when he got tired of beating me up. My father took me home, iced my face and told me he was proud of me. 'You're no coward.'

He believed in dressing well. 'Just because we don't have money doesn't mean we can't look good,' he used to tell me. And he himself looked pretty good in an adult way, which was probably how he snared my unsuspecting mother. He taught me how to tie a Windsor knot. Dapper.

When I told him about wanting to invite Chink to a Central-Girls mixer he seemed relieved. All of my buddies had already been going out with girls.

'So you've got a girlfriend finally?'

'No, she's just a friend.'

'Well, that's a start.'

'She plays violin in the orchestra.'

'Not bad. What does she see in you?'

'Cut it out, Dad. Like I said, we're just friends.'

I walked her home after the dance and held her hand. Her mother invited me in for a cup of tea and I was surprised at how nice and how normal she behaved: she didn't look at all drunk, despite being Irish. But she looked tired. It must have been hard raising two kids on her own, especially when one of them, Viola, was so attractive and she had to go to work, unlike all the other mothers I knew.

'So did you get to first base?' asked my dad, puffing away.

'I'm in the on-deck circle, pops.'

'Don't call me pops, I'm your father.'

'Okay, Dad, sorry.'

He's funny that way, and in other ways as well. For example, he would say things like 'Sometimes a cigar is just a cigar,' which is something I never questioned: what else could it be?

My mom wasn't so enthusiastic about my having a friend who was a girl.

'You should be doing your studies.'

'I *am* doing my studies. I'm an A student, Mom.'

'Yeah, but for how long? Do you want to end up like your father?'

I went to my room.

Chink and I never had any real dates. We rode up and back to school together on the subway and took walks in the park on weekends. She spent a lot of time practicing her violin and I spent a lot of time mooning at her, at her slim arms and slender neck, desperate to kiss her yet never making a move. At home I imagined all sorts of scenarios that would lead to the goal and ransacked Shakespeare for hints but the light of day squelched them. We talked, though, about every little nothing, and the big things too, like how she missed her dad, a career Marine who got killed in the stupid Vietnam War, and how she was worried about her mom who scraped together the money to get her started on the fiddle to give her something to do besides crying for her dad.

'Were they happy?'

'I think so. What about your folks?'

'They spend a lot of time not being with each other.'

When we ran out of words she pulled out her fiddle and played strange music and began to ask me if I liked certain phrases. Over summer vacation we kept in touch and I took it in my head to get a guitar with the earnings from my job on an ice cream truck. She was delighted that after a few weeks I was already able to strum a dozen different chords and could accompany her, sort of. We had big plans for the next year at school: I was keen to join the drama club and she would be able to take individual violin lessons and try out for solo parts with the orchestra.

When we did kiss, finally, on a remote park bench behind a thicket near the tennis courts, it was painful, because we both knew that with the kiss came all the burning complexities of wanting more of each other. But we kept kissing anyway, sometimes for hours. Once I tried getting to second base and she slapped me so hard my ears began to ring. But she let me kiss her again.

We explored the city during the long hot hours of the summer, taking the bus into town after our part-time jobs, splurging on the cheap but good cafeteria coffee at the main library where we borrowed books by the cartloads, books just half-begun because we found our own ideas far more intriguing. She wondered why there had to be twelve notes to a scale when there could be an infinite number of tones, and she showed me on the violin how the most minute movement up or down a string produced a different pitch. I argued that making poetry was far harder than making music because with music, see, anyone could create a lovely phrase and it could mean virtually anything, but words were unforgiving, they were specific, and the secret of poetry was to make words seem like music. Then we both agreed that music could be made without either words or sounds – and started kissing.

We spent as little time at our homes as possible. I felt sorry for my parents – did they ever kiss?

And Chink now had to weather a new development: her mom had a boyfriend. Part of her was relieved – for her mom; and part of her rebelled at the notion of a displacement of her dad, no matter how dead he was.

The new guy seemed very nice and her mom so full of life that it made her scared. But in no time at all he had moved in and the tenor quickly changed. It was all too sudden: once he felt the comfort of a berth, home became a place of quiet unease for Chink. He made a few creepy comments about her older sister and what was worse, he started to ridicule her violin. When she fought back he brought down the hammer: no more practicing when he was there. He didn't like it. Period. He wanted to watch TV in peace. Chink's mom didn't make a peep, which was the most unkindest cut of all.

I'd never seen a person fall apart, but there was no mistake: Chink was falling apart. She cried all the time, in my arms and out. It was so bad I thought she would have to go to Byberry. I had no idea what to do, nowhere to turn, so I talked to my father.

'What kind of man wouldn't be proud of a kid who plays violin?' he grumbled in disgust. 'What's he like, who is he?'

'He's one of us, Dad.'

'What do you mean one of us?'

'Italian.'

'You mean a stupid guinea, not one of us.'

'Don't get involved,' said my mother, who had stolen downstairs, 'it's none of your business. What do you expect from the Irish?'

'The Irish, Mom, what do you mean the Irish? The guy's a dago!' I yelled.

'And the mother? What kind of mother lets a man take over her home like that? And they're not even married! Nice example for her children. No wonder the older one's running around like a whore. The whole neighbourhood knows about her. But the mother at least should have more sense. Not even married.'

It was no use arguing with Mom. My father shrugged his shoulders and took out a cigar.

'Let me think a little.'

Saturday morning my father rose early and decked himself out in a three-piece beige suit, beautifully cut, with all the trimmings: cufflinks, monogrammed shirt, silk tie (Windsor knot!) and matching breast-pocket handkerchief. He looked like a million bucks. Then to top it all off he got his Homburg.

'Where do you think you're going?' cried my mom.

'For a walk. Come on, chief.'

I knew something was up. We went over to the other side of our neighbourhood, the poor side and straight to Chink's home. Christ, what was the old man up to? He knocked on the door. Her mother answered.

'Hello, Mrs. Cingolini,' said Dad, doffing his hat. 'You've already met my son. I'm his father. May we come in and have a word with you?'

'Who's there honey?' called a rough voice from the bedroom.

'Olivia's friend,' she answered, adding after a pause, 'and his father.'

'Who?'

Chink ran out and stared at us. She was haggard, all eighty pounds of her, and red-eyed.

The boyfriend emerged in a tee-shirt and jeans, with bare feet. He was a big guy who hadn't bothered to shave for a few days.

My dad turned to Chink and asked her to bring him her violin. The boyfriend was too startled to react.

'May we sit down, Mrs. Cingolini?' asked Dad. He emphasised the "Mrs."

We seated ourselves at the kitchen table.

'What do you two bozos want? Is this the kid who's been fiddling around with Ollie?' the boyfriend sniggered.

My father tensed ever so slightly but ignored the remark as he took Chink's fiddle with a kind of sure-handed reverence. I had seen my father get angry, really angry, just once, and it wasn't a pretty sight: his anger was the soft hair-raising kind, which is hard for me to explain, but it made you break out in a sweat. I could see he was getting there again. He cleared his throat and spoke barely above a whisper. He took care to enunciate every word.

'You see, mister whoever-you-are, sometimes a violin is more than a violin. One of my associates,' and here Dad placed a small card onto the table with a snap like he was dealing trump, 'likes to use violins for purposes other than making music.'

The boyfriend lost all colour, collapsed into a chair like an unstrung puppet and started to babble.

'*Zitto*!' Dad commanded. He was no longer whispering. 'If I *ever* hear that you've kept this precious daughter of Mrs. Cingolini from playing her violin at any time of the day or night, or if I *ever* hear that you've laid a hand on her, her sister or their mother – *ever!* – this violin will be the last thing you see.'

My father rose. 'Thank you, Mrs. Cingolini. May I have your permission to escort Olivia to my home? Your daughter has volunteered to play a few tunes for me, and my son will accompany her on guitar.'

The boarder split, Mom is spending a lot less time in bed, Olivia and I are officially going out and Dad, well, Dad decided to give up cigars and take up the violin. Now that's what I call ambition.

Violin Caprice No. 21

She sat in her stylist's chair gazing from half-closed eyes at the apparition of a very beautiful face. It gave her great satisfaction, this face, and she observed it keenly, as she would a rival's. The comforting pressure of the stylist's hands and the efficient flamboyance of the scissors dancing around her head generated a smile. Sweet chemical scents worked on her as an elixir that banished all illegitimate but tenacious concerns about the rest of her body, particularly the circumference of her thighs.

She was young and still much engaged in the struggle to rid herself of flaws, weaknesses, limitations, and defects of body and of character. She had not yet reached the age when their inexorability begins to be felt and out of panic are trumpeted and displayed as strengths and virtues. She was further still from the time when such repugnancies, like familiar warts, create no disturbance whatsoever in consciousness because they have been woven so thoroughly and seamlessly into one's accepted notion of self.

In the beginning there was no need for caution. Mark's subtle praise had vanquished her. Flush with the exquisite victory conferred by having captured the attentions of a learned man more than twice her age, she allowed herself to revel and bloom. She fearlessly converted his first physical advances, awkwardly tentative by design, into the avant garde of love. She ignored all signs that betrayed the carefully studied aspect of the seduction, all the small hesitancies of Mark's speech, all the charming self-deprecations he placed at her feet to provide her with the enchanting power of gracious dismissal.

But he went too far. It was a careless act of his that converted blindness into vision, like a lightning bolt betraying momentarily the obscured features of a landscape. Thus despite all impetus to believe in him and his love and consequently a love for herself and her capabilities, the eerie momentary flash could not be erased.

She recalled the moment while her long lovely hair was being clipped and curled into ringlets. She recalled how Mark, thinking she was asleep, stood motionless above the bed where she lay. His hair was wet. Joann saw him glance at the table where her most recent attempt at poetry resided, and she saw him smirk, briefly, sufficiently, confirming what she had known but refused to believe until then, that her poetry was academically informed trash. She now realised that the entire emotional history of her life had been short-changed by the poetic mauling it had suffered, and she realised too that Mark had been encouraging her to mangle what she held so dear.

Martin wheeled suddenly away from the keyboard, deftly obliterating from the screen any trace of his writing. He was startled to see Diana's head in the doorway as if she had leapt from his new story, and sat immobilised until the jarring male voice corrected his imagination.

'I hope I haven't disturbed you, Professor, but the front door was open.' It was Jeremy, one of Martin's more intelligent students, one of his fans.

'I'm beginning to think you're rather impertinent, Jeremy,' said Martin, trying to appear irritated. Diana would not be back until evening. 'I suppose you want to talk about paronomasias.'

'Well,' said Jeremy suavely, 'I really wanted to follow up on a few matters you raised in the lecture series.'

'I raised more than a few, I think.'

'Yes, and a lot of us were quite uplifted by what you had to say.'

'Perhaps,' said Martin gravely, 'you should get to the point.' He rose and strode over to the young man and kissed him firmly on the lips.

Several hours later, after Jeremy had been dismissed, Martin took exquisite pleasure in examining his face. It was not the face of Alexander or Caesar, but he had joined their ranks in his own small way.

The interlude with Jeremy lasted several months and ended with the semester. Jeremy was satisfied with his grade, and not being constitutionally homosexual, took up again easily with an old girlfriend. Martin's reputation was garnished by a scandal openly overlooked by university administration and openly admired by students for its flouting of convention. Here after all was one liberated humanist. Diana too was admired: for her sophistication.

Despite every better impulse Diana simply could not wrench herself away from him. He knew, after all, nearly every detail of importance about her life: her parents' early inexplicable divorce, the imposing nature of her stepfather, the unnaturally quiet adolescence, and the desperate leap into poetry as a way of making sense out of an unknown self. Most disturbingly he knew of certain fleeting sensations she had experienced, much more comprehensively depicted in her naive and spontaneous chatter rather than her literary work, sensations affecting the entire body and mind. Ultimately ineffable, they nevertheless seemed to Diana as sturdy and pertinent to the crafting of a life as food. In the first months of her being with Martin, lying with back pressed to his substantial reassuring paunch, she had babbled about these dim intimations of childhood ecstasies and their connection to images of absolute pastoral stillness and light. Somehow it always came out rather trite, but she knew with certainty this was an inevitable distortion because the onrush of energies provided by these rare episodes was so tangible, so pregnant with chances for happiness, however inchoate. Martin explained it away by quoting himself: to him it was the 'blissful boundaryless love of man for Man' that pervaded the work of the great.

But her life now was fairly shabby. She endured Martin's theoretical excursions about love and potentiality, she endured Jeremy's impertinence, and she kept clinging, hoping that Martin's strong hands would obliterate the weakness of her own character, never more evident than when she allowed herself, in the company of Jeremy, to be introduced to Martin's daughter as friends whom he wished his daughter would someday not only accept but grow close to.

It was months since this humiliating debacle. Jeremy had gone and she and Martin had resumed their familiar academic ways together. Martin's new story, featuring a principal character suspiciously resembling her, had been accepted for publication. His campus stature was therefore immense and he bore up admirably under the strain of accolades. Diana for her part was paralysed: she sensed the hard ugly chill in Martin, and knew nothing permanent could come of a life with him, but for the moment she could find no alternative. She rejected outright the attentions of men more her age: a project of slow mutual growth with a stranger was unthinkable. She lost weight without attempting to.

'Martin,' she began timidly one evening, 'how's your daughter?'

Without missing a peck of the computer keys Martin replied that it was really something he wished not to discuss.

'Why not?' she persevered.

'Because I would prefer not to,' he answered, adding superciliously, 'just like Bartleby. Or don't you read Melville?'

'You've changed,' she commented sadly.

Martin pursed his lips angrily.

'When are you going to expand that bourgeois mind of yours and be thankful for a little liberation? What do you want from me?'

'I don't think you've been fair, Martin.'

'All right, tell me I've been using you. Guess what, we all use each other. That's life. Don't blame me because you can't write anymore.'

'That isn't it and it isn't just me, though I used to think I could be happy being your little slut-poet.'

'Don't you dare denigrate my feelings for you!' Martin shouted.

Diana smiled and went on. 'I used to think I could be happy just *being* with you, and I could have, and I still could be, if you tell me what happened, what happened to you. You're a big deal here, the books, the students you have, but even stupid me can see you hate yourself for something, that your heart's not in this bullshit. It can't be.'

Martin lifted his right hand and rubbed his forefinger and thumb together in front of his face.

'Do you know what this is?'

Diana, somewhere between rage and befuddlement, simply stared.

'No, of course you wouldn't. I'll tell you: it's the world's smallest violin, and it's playing a very sad melody, just for you.'

The surface of Diana's face trembled like an ice sheet on a mountain slope about to cascade. Her gaunt emaciated figure in the falling light frightened and stirred the man.

'Come here,' he said softly. She came. He kissed her forehead. 'Maybe you really do love me.'

Diana began to cry and mutely affirm her assent. 'Well, my darling, love requires sacrifice.'

He stroked her long long hair for several minutes while cradling her head in his lap as she knelt before him. He then eased a pair of scissors from the writing table into his hand and methodically began to crop her tresses. Diana's meekness infuriated him, so the scissors worked ever closer to the scalp, leaving in their wake a ragged patchwork terrain like unkempt pasture.

When Diana peered into the bathroom mirror she smiled. Without a word she gathered up the long strands of her hair and spent the rest of the night braiding and knotting them into a coil six feet in length. She carefully placed the noose, her first real work of art, on the pillow next to Martin's head while he slept. Then she left.

Violin Caprice No. 22

I can much better describe my childhood with the furling of melodic lines and the fashioning of harmonic tapestries through aural space-time as, for example, I've already done to some extent in *Still Quiring* and *Breath Upon the Bank*. Words, alas, have their place, although they are far poorer than pure music. When we composers reach out to attain the impossible, as any composer should and must, we often have recourse to fool's gold, believing that the union of word with pitched sound enhances when in fact it becomes a travesty. 'All men will be brothers!' – how trite! What a confession of failure for the symphonist to resort to these cheap clap-trap tricks. On the very very rare occasion when I will allow myself to venture beyond the first three sublime, if archaic, movements of the Ninth, I shiver in disappointment. And opera ...

I tried my hand, having accepted a lucrative commission from a wealthy Mahlerite (or is it Mahlerian?) who was convinced by an obscure Spanish psychologist that the drama of Mahler's meeting with Sigmund Freud in Leyden, Holland in 1910 was the stuff of majestic tragedy. I did my home-work: I listened to the interminably plaintive *cri de coeur* that was Mahler; I threw myself into the intersecting lives of the ostensibly beautiful Alma, the impetuous and brilliant archi-tect Walter Gropius and the composer himself sequestered in his summertime Alpine hut; mused upon the fiery maudlin infidelities and swoons; and I entertained the Spaniard's thesis that Mahler's choice to love his errant spouse marked the end of his creative and, shortly thereafter, literal life. The result: musical comedy, a delightful farce! The rich man who commissioned me was infuriated and paid treble my fee to forestall a New York premiere. Little did he know that all opera becomes musical farce, inescapable because of the grafting of words onto a host that cannot abide, invasive and unwanted strangers in the strange land of music.

My parents were Jewish, though strictly atheist and with communist leanings they kept carefully hidden; they were idealists too, and poor. I've come to realise that poverty has no redeeming features. I've come to understand that one does not have to be poor to be idealistic. But I'm grateful for the lessons of an early childhood rich in poverty. That's not very funny, is it? I'm not very good with words, as I warned you, because my world has been a world of sound from as long ago as I can recall.

The opening interval of "Frère Jacques" seemed uncannily like the pitch difference of my mother's heartbeat: *Frère* Jacques, *Frère* Jacques, *Frère* Jacques.... I spent long nights lying awake and listening for every creak and shudder in our small apartment, the scurrying of mouse feet across the uneven wooden floors, the wind against the windowpane, the occasional startled cry of a cat – or a person, the listless mass of moving air created by passing cars, the stirrings from my parents' bed, all scintillating like aural fireworks.

I spoke little as a child, suspicious of the crudity and specificity of words, and I sang without them. When I first saw and heard a piano at kindergarten my parents had to pry me away in tears: at last, a way to reproduce, only approximately of course, the din within! I consider my explorations of the piano at the time as artistically genuine as anything I subsequently composed.

My musical world, with or without piano, was endlessly intriguing, far far more than the world of other children and adults, the world of eating, pinching, fighting, seeing, the world in which I was an active participant – on the outside – while on the inside I hummed with running harmonies. I'm amused at the description of childhood as an age of innocence: we would have murdered each other many times over in fits of pique had we the capability. To tease and be teased was constant – and yet here I am grateful, because teasing is just what music does, increasing energy and releasing, seducing and letting go: it has been the essence of my work.

I was possessed by sound and sound was the medium for me to translate what I perceived and what I felt: sound was, in fact, feeling. I really had no choice but to make music and so I organised by life in obeisance to this implacable fact.

Because my deprecation of the ordinary was so apparent my parents took me to a special doctor, bearded and menacing, who convinced them to give me pills. I was seven years old at the time and on the third night of pill-taking, as I lay in bed listening and hearing, my body seized as if a cramp had overtaken every limb, my neck twisted and my eyes screwed sideways and upwards. When I went to scream I had no voice. My mother, happening upon me before she retired, nearly became a Believer (in Satan). No more pills after that, ever, even though a few enemies, rivals, have suggested I need them.

By an accident of genes I was, and am, very beautiful. Once in high school I decided I'd had enough of ostracism and teasing from the girls who confused physical beauty with some sort of talent, so I dressed up just like the prettiest ones in magazines, did my hair like them, made up my face with foundation, eye-shadow and rouge and sauntered into class. That earned me a great deal of envy and fear: the teasing stopped. Fortunately for them boys held little interest for me then.

The musical side of school was a haven. I excelled at the piano which I always knew was merely an "instrument" – I strove to use it for my own expressive devices, not to perform on it, if you know what I mean. When the violin was introduced I had the great good sense to stay away: one could lose one's life in devotion to its infinite tonalities, in striving for the impossible task of "mastering" it – as if one could master such a seductress!

I reached college after a disastrous year at a conservatory for which I had been awarded a full scholarship. It was the most miserable and excruciating year of my young life: they tried to "teach" me to compose! They insisted on rules, strictures, formulas and templates when form itself was anathema to me, so I transferred out before they ruined me. At university the music department was wise enough to leave me to my own devices. They were grateful that I, a female composer of serious music, and therefore as rare as a hen's tooth, actually *composed*, fluidly and prolifically, whereas nearly everyone else agonised to produce a few paltry notes.

By the time I graduated I had reached op. 43. To be fair most of my compositions were brief, miniatures of no more than five minutes in duration, for I preferred concision. One of my professors implored me to write a sonata. 'Why?' I responded. I was answering to the dictates and directions of an irrepressible source within. As my expressive abilities grew I discovered the tremendously exhausting ecstasy of giving an ever more exact approximation to the music I couldn't help but hear, followed by a restive state of dissatisfaction. In that lull, when even the most creative mind wonders whether it has emptied itself forever, a riot of sensual yearning overwhelmed me, and only then did I discover boys. They were easy enough to acquire because of my beauty, and easy to lose when they recognised that my passion even at its most intense was quite impersonal, no matter how exciting or satisfying. I wanted what animated them from beyond.

Music is neither moral nor immoral: it is trans-moral. My life in service to music could not be constrained. To continue to compose, which was for me as essential as breathing, I realised that I required support, and support eventually arrived in the form of a smart handsome lawyer five years older with a penchant for the arts. He was a man who claimed to have been moved by something in my works – and why should I have disbelieved him? – and who agreed to dedicate himself to them, through me. He also secretly fancied himself a Gauguin, just waiting for an explosion of talent after his obligatory preliminaries with money-making. I might easily have entered a lucrative profession such as medicine or the law, but I knew with certainty that my musical daemon would not have survived. I was very clear about the conditions of marriage and about the demands made upon me by my art: no children, and no strictures.

As a consequence our marriage was a success. We liked each other, we got along, we made an attractive couple and I found that his presence, affable and witty, buffered me at social events. He gave me what I needed most to answer to my cause, and I appreciated it, earning a small amount of fame as my reputation grew and as my works became known to that very small scattered minority who appreciated their strange appealing dissonances and dream-like textures.

One day I received a commission from a representative of a violinist who, tired of Tartini, wished to have at his disposal a concerto for violin and orchestra in three movements: The Devil's Grin, The Devil's Laughter and The Devil's Silence. The commission stipulated that the violinist's ideas would first be imparted to the composer via a third party and that the violinist would remain anonymous until the completion of the work, at which point he – I suspected a "he" but that may have been pure prejudice – would give his blessing, or not. If he were not satisfied, I would keep only half the fee and of course I was free to do as I wished with the piece.

I was about to reject this silly proposition out of hand, for I could never bring myself to write a "virtuoso" piece for any instrument, let alone one so ill-used as the violin. But the idea of the demonic, a quality I sensed was one from which I had shied away in my music to date, intrigued. Could this be the catalyst for my crossing the Rubicon, for my reaching beyond the veil? I wasn't beholden to any particular constraint, except for a tripartite division. I agreed.

Within a fortnight I received a missive: "The Devil grins when he sees the Lord's subject swearing virtue."

I set to work immediately and was astonished by the outflow of easy natural dancing lightness amidst a transparent orchestral undulation out of which the violin cavorted with just enough of a hint of the sinister, all culminating in a unnervingly lush slightly discordant *tutti*. The technical demands for the violinist were tonal rather than athletic.

Several weeks later another message arrived: "The Devil laughs when sinners take pleasure in evil."

An orgy of percussive colour ensued, a whirl of cacophonous asperity sweetened by a sheer beauty of melodic fragments into and around which the violin lent a frenetic mirth. The soloist would have to be a veritable Paganini to execute the movement accurately. I was breathless with what I had achieved, and fearful. The musical imperatives that flooded me were unfamiliar.

I awaited my final instruction with trepidation, and a month later I hastily ripped open the envelope to read: "The Devil is silent when the Creator rests."

Here I attained the truly sublime, beginning the movement with a vast incandescent cackling, like leaping fires, which swelled to a diaphanous mist, the gossamer violin meandering in the subtlest of frenzied capers, barely audible, until the swell and fires subsided into a nothingness represented by the lone instrument's golden slides in the uppermost of its registers.

I was exhausted, spent as I had never been, possessed by a physical restlessness that could not be assuaged by the usual means. Weeks passed during which I – changed. I became angry, anxious, tearful at times and, most surprising, even vocal. I raged at my useless spouse for his humility and the few friends I possessed bore witness to my unbounded sarcasm as I assaulted their bourgeois sensibilities. I took lonely jaunts to the city ghettos, verifying the sordid and inhaling the putrid. Most worrisomely, the sounds that typically returned to propel me to something new had not reappeared. As I awaited the violinist's verdict I suffered.

At last I had my answer: approval, a cheque, and a request to meet: would I come to such and such a hotel on such and such a night? But still no name! Who could it be? Who would have both the money and the technique?

I flew there and was admitted to a luxurious suite where I met – her! She was young and making a name for herself, pretty but hardly stunning. She had a reputation for exceptional proficiency, but her career was fledgling. I was puzzled. She looked uncommonly haughty.

'I think you'll need a glass of wine,' she said. 'You've written a masterpiece: congratulations. May I try some things out for you?'

She played excerpts from each of the movements, ending with the breathtaking final passage. She exceeded my expectations. She replaced her violin and addressed me.

'This is a work that will make you famous, I have no doubt, and me as well. It will do wonders for my career. But there is a story behind it and you will have a choice to make.'

She rose and leaned towards me.

'Your docile husband and I are lovers, and have been for several years. Does that surprise you? It shouldn't. While you have been living in your immaterial world I have grown to love him, and he me.'

I was stupefied and enraged, but I hardly knew how to respond, so I merely gulped the remainder of my wine. She replenished my glass.

'You can have him back – on one and only one condition. That you allow me to claim ownership of your score. It is, after all, far different from your other works, and I myself have composed a bit. To bring it out under my name would be a welcome and much-needed coup for an aspiring soloist like me. You have a choice.'

So here was the very Devil herself. I grinned, laughed, and then became silent.

'No. Take him,' I eventually replied.

And so she did, and on the strength of my Devil's Concerto grew famous and much admired – but not as a composer. At the premiere my ex-husband gazed rapturously as she performed but nodded furtively, as if with gratitude, to me.

The rest, of course, is silence. I composed no longer: the sounds ceased within after the ultimate sacrifice, for I had come to realise I had really loved the man, and in that moment chose most wisely for him.

Violin Caprice No. 23

'Okay, Jimbo, you tell me if this is kosher.'

Manny handed the opera glasses to his partner, aka "The Barometer," the two of them inconspicuous in the crowd of earnest admirers, all with that facial sheen of insipid adoration. Jimbo spotted a blonde and leggy looker who leapt out of the sea of shabby to her feet just as the bum at the podium finished reading a story, screaming her head off. On the other side of the auditorium, almost perfectly in synch, a pimply-faced teenage boy did the same. Naturally the cretins followed their lead and it was yet another standing ovation.

'They're plants, Manny.'

'Tell me about it. But who are they? Every show, here, Europe, even Down Under, it's the same. They're connected, but we can't figure out how – at least not yet.'

'Let me work on it.'

'Work fast, Jimbo: we're running outta time.'

They listened to the so-called author drone on again in that peculiar expressionless voice. It just didn't make sense. The guy doesn't tweet, twit, whatever, he's not on Facebook, his jokes, if you can call them jokes, are weird, and he's definitely no Jack Benny, not by a long shot. But he's packing them in, big time, big houses. He's not even a goddamned preacher.

The Barometer sighed. He'd been on the case for three months: nothing, nada, zip. The jerk was clean as a whistle to boot, but maybe, just maybe … The "show," which was nothing more than a reading, imagine that, was over, and the audience was now stomping and whistling, pleading for an encore, like they all did. The blonde and the pimply kid were gone. Very suspicious.

Two days later Manny strolled into Jimbo's office, a big smile creasing his mug.

'Take a look at this.' He tossed a slip of paper to Jimbo who read with glee. 'An overdue library book: that psychopathic son of a bitch!' he exclaimed.

'Wait, Jimbo, there's more.'

Manny produced a printout of the Perp's borrowings for the past three years.

'Are you ready? Here: de Courcy, Auer, Boscassi, Fetis, Hill, Sacconi, Roth, Mozart, L., Schoenberg, Mantovani, Sugden, Shaw. Now throw in the CDs and DVDs: Heifetz, Kreisler, Milstein, Elman, Seidel, Joachim, Menuhin, Ysaÿe, Accardo, Ricci, Friedman, Zukerman (no relation to Bernie), Szeryng – way too many to list – and there's definitely a thread.'

'There's more than a thread, Manny, the guy's obsessed.' They didn't call Jimbo "The Barometer" for nothing.

'I guess that's what being a perv is all about,' reflected Manny.

Meanwhile Interpol and the FBI were meeting in Manhattan comparing notes. They had been tracking the Perp and compiling a list of the mystery cheerleaders, nearly sixty of them, a sordid international collection of reprobates: doctors, lawyers, teachers, philosophers, gaybirds, various musicians (mainly violinists), boxers, grifters, communists, anarchists, buskers, novelists, Italians, accountants, Jews, poets, fetishists, even a tribal chief of some kind, but also – and this was hard to swallow – kids and dogs. A goddamned cult with a few too many gorgeous dolls. And it was growing. Bernie Zukerman, the lead FBI agent on the case, was beginning to lose it, screaming at his Interpol counterpart, Emile Zingarello, who screamed back. The regally debonair and aristocratic European had to be pried away from the slovenly but feisty Brooklyn cop who had toughed his way up the ranks. Bernie's partners calmed him down but Emile's handlers threatened to walk. Frayed nerves were the norm when the Agencies hit a brick wall, but reason eventually prevailed: given the stakes, it couldn't afford not to. Emile offered his hand and Bernie shook, though he nearly went at it again when the European moved in for a peck on the cheek. Finally they got down to comparing notes.

'Let's start with the ladies, shall we? Isabella, Mandy, Joan – Christ, doesn't anybody have a surname?' asked Bernie.

'We are doing the best we can, sir,' replied Emile unctuously. 'But these people are wily, devious, and they know how to cover their tracks. They've been *very* well trained, very well trained. Still, my men have come up with a number of leads: Ricci, Tesi, Cingolini, Jones, Schwarz, Eisenman, Seltzerlust, Hummel, Squillace, Menard, Kikinski, Martin, Sol and Sarcophagus.'

'Sarcophagus? Are you pulling my chain?'

'No, sir, it's been verified.'

'Alright, let's get to work. I want every scrap of information – *everything* – bus tickets, laundry receipts, anything and everything on these characters, do you hear me?'

'Naturally, we are quite thorough on the Continent,' replied Emile, and the way he said it you knew he was taking a dig at the Americans, but Bernie didn't bite.

'We'll let Manny and The Barometer know. Now let's pray they can crack this nut.'

* * *

At the mention of the overdue book, a so-called mystery about a stolen Stradivarius, the Perp began to tremble.

'You just can't get enough, can you?' scoffed Manny, dripping with contempt.

'I was going to return it today, I swear!'

'Shut up, you lying son of a bitch!' Jimbo couldn't contain himself.

'Hold on, kemosabe,' soothed Manny, 'I'll take over.'

He signalled for the Perp to ease himself into the Lay-Z-Boy.

'We want you to feel relaxed.' Manny smiled but there was fire in his gut.

'Looks like you've got a thing for violins.' It was out there now, hanging heavily over the Perp's head.

'Actually, I do, I think ... '

'We know what you think,' broke in The Barometer, 'you perverted bastard.' Manny had to restrain him.

'Please forgive my friend,' he said to the Perp. 'He often gets carried away. But let's begin with the violin. Believe me,' he urged smoothly, 'if you come clean it'll be a lot easier. Tell me.'

'I like the violin.'

'Yeah, we know how much you like the violin. A whole hell of a lot, huh?'

'I guess you could say that.'

'Of course we can say it.' Manny leaned in, his coffee breath hitting the Perp's face like a slap. 'But what's the game?'

'Huh?'

'The game,' repeated Manny sharply, 'what are you up to?'

'Let me at him, Manny,' exclaimed Jimbo, foaming at the mouth with rage.

Manny checked his partner once again and then Jimbo handed him a piece of paper.

'Let's jog your memory a bit: do any of these names ring a bell? Eisenman, Jones, Menard – to name a few.'

'Why, yes, they're all … '

'They're all part of your sick cult, that's what they are!' shouted The Barometer. 'We're gonna nail your sorry ass to the cross!'

'Cool it, Jimbo, he's just not worth it,' said Manny, struggling to keep The Barometer at bay. He then turned to the Perp. 'I can hold him back only so long, so tell me – tell *us* – how you do it, how you get a bunch of strangers to pay to listen to that sick crap you purvey, tell us about Kikinski and Schwarz and the others, tell us about the goddamned dogs, okay? Spill it – *now* before it's too late. We've got ways to make creeps like you give it up,' he added ominously.

'It's hard to … '

'That's it, enough!' shouted Manny. 'Don't say you didn't ask for it, tough guy!'

Jimbo strutted over and popped a CD into the sound system. Sweat laced the Perp's brow as the music of Andre Rieu poured out of the loudspeakers.

'What's wrong, I thought you liked violin music?' cackled Jimbo. Manny joined in, but after a minute both men grew alarmed: they had gone too far too soon. The Perp was crying in agony, a huddled heap of jelly. They might lose him before he could be useful, and that would look bad, very bad – so they cut off the track. The softie's sobs began to subside, but he was still a heaving mess. Manny fetched him a cup of water and slowly, very slowly, he came round, breathing heavily.

'I, I thought, I wished,' he stammered, 'I wanted to write a few things to amuse myself, a few pieces, miniature stories really, all of which had something to do with my favourite instrument, the violin, which I did. It was just for myself, just a way to relax, that's all, I swear! And then a few friends asked about what I was doing, and so I shared them, tentatively at first. Now other people seem to like them.'

The Perp's parched lips made speaking difficult. Jimbo opened the door: no use pushing him over the brink, even if they didn't believe a word the lying sonofabitch said. They sighed for the good old days when evidence was what you got *after* you took care of the criminal. It was time to see Bernie.

In Manhattan Bernie and Emile briefed Manny and The Barometer. 'Nothing new, except we know Eisenman's dead, most of the women are knockouts and the violinists, male and female, are like fighter pilots: wild and cocky, even the youngest of them.'

'But how do we put it all together?'

'Simple: he's working the System against itself. He's an Occupier, a revolutionary, he's trying to wean simple decent people away from television and the movies, the no-good subversive. And then what? I'll tell you: all of a sudden you've got a bunch of ordinary folk, salt of the earth, who want more – more music, more poetry, more words! Soon they'll be ungovernable, soon they'll be laughing quietly in that sick sort of "I'm enjoying a bit of fun and wit" way; soon the entire fabric of Western culture will be ripped to shreds. How does a half-empty Super Bowl sound?'

Jimbo pulled on his jacket, zipped it up, corralled a few Hershey bars and addressed his colleagues.

'Somebody's got to take the plunge. Don't try to stop me – if I'm not back tomorrow by this time, you'll know what happened.'

Manny went white. Bernie and Emile gulped and saluted The Barometer as he strode off with a determined intention that would brook no compromise. No, he'd go it alone to the source.

It was a nerve-wracking night and day for the troops. Emile couldn't put down the aqua minerale, Bernie was popping sugarless gum like candy and Manny nearly drowned himself in decaf. Would Jimbo make it? The door swung open and there he was! The Barometer!

But something was different, something small but telling. Jimbo carefully laid the Perp's book on Bernie's desk and smoothed it with his hand. He looked as if he'd just gotten to his feet after a haymaker.

'Jimbo, are you okay?' asked Manny.

'Am I okay? Sure I'm okay!'

Bernie was sceptical.

'So ... '

'So I made it through them, all twenty-four,' Jimbo said dreamily. 'Now I understand, gentlemen, now I understand. I'm still not sure how he does it, but he makes these characters come alive. And more: he makes me ... '

Jimbo excused himself for a moment. He returned with a violin case, the hard old fashioned kind. Manny, Bernie and Emile, taken unawares and foolishly unarmed, put their hands up: they weren't expecting this, not from one of their own.

'Hold on, buddy,' pleaded Manny, 'we're on the same team!'

The Barometer smiled deviously and popped open the lid.

Then Manny, Bernie and Emile, glancing incredulously at each other brought their hands down quickly to cover their ears while Jimbo started to saw away, oblivious as an airport Hare Krishna with a tambourine, another lost soul down the tubes.

Violin Caprice No. 24

Choosing the *Capricci* for his farewell recital was inspired. His last performance of the lot of these insanely demanding "miniatures" coincided with personal events whose resonance had ebbed but would never diminish to silence even as he had forged onwards to his various successes and rewards, which were considerable, as distinguished chamber musician, soloist and teacher. Yes, the *Capricci* were ideal for him now as he bowed out to avert the ignominy of discovering, one day in performance, that one's musical desires could not be approximated by one's musical technique.

Like virtually every talented violinist he had attacked the *Capricci* in his youth as if they were Alpine training exercises for an assault on Everest. But in time their charm – how else might he describe it? – won him over and now, although he could never admit such heresy in public, he preferred them to anything written for solo violin by Bach, though musically they remained a mystery. It was to this mystery he had given himself six months of preparation: a nice way, thought Matteo Beauvoir, to add a flourish to his career and to launch what would probably be the final phase of his sometimes messy but always interesting journey to nothingness.

His teaching duties were far from onerous. Over the years he had mellowed considerably and aside from small matters of technique he now made it a rule never to dictate, often saying things like 'Play it however you like, try to get all the notes, and then see what you think.' He'd also begun to enjoy, surprising himself immensely, introducing children to the incomparable sound of a bowed violin, leaping at every community outreach programme available and bustling about in the cramped urban classrooms like a dervish. A few of his colleagues were appalled when he handed his Guarnerius del Gesù to a five year old to strum like a guitar. 'It's just a glorified cigar box,' he quipped.

As for his life outside music, and he seriously wondered whether life could indeed exist outside music, he'd had his share of emotional complexity and aside perhaps from one decision, no regrets, and even there, if regret meant wanting to do something differently, he wasn't sure. Maybe that's what regret really was all about: not being sure.

He took his own pedagogical advice to heart as he approached the *Capricci* anew, interested not so much in the outrageous stretches required – up to a twelfth! – or the impossible double trills, three-and four-string chords, tumbling spiccato, left hand pizzicato, fingered octaves, flying staccato and undulating or ricochet bowing – but in what these were meant to evoke. And now, at age sixty-two, as he contemplated the scores and made his way through them at the slowest possible pace, which heightened perception, he began to grin.

There was tragedy, silliness, eerie demonism, suffering, vertiginous ecstasy, melancholy, anguish, mockery, triumph, perhaps even heroism, but above all there was love, that's the only way he could describe it: weird perhaps and often occult, but unmistakeable. In Paganini, the so-called devil! And wasn't it interesting, he mused further, that music, the greatest of arts, could express every facet of the human condition except one? There was, is, and can be no musical language for evil – that was the domain of words. No, the very essence of music was love, which in words was ever elusive and indefinable, like a subatomic particle whose existence might only be inferred but never directly observed. Maybe outside music only the corrupted forms of love could be found.

Well, it wouldn't be a note-perfect night, and Matteo doubted that Paganini himself would have been capable of flawless execution, at least not for the entire set at one go. The small hall, chosen for its exceptional acoustics, was full and Matteo entered with nonchalance. Pausing at centre stage he departed from convention – his convention, at least – in thanking the attendees and speaking about the life of Paganini, with emphasis on the physical illnesses he endured, taking care to cast an eye on the furthest rows and discovering to his relief that she was there.

The bariolage of the first capriccio set the tone, creating a web of never quite disappearing chords, uncannily like life, a glowing aural foundation for the devilish intensities to follow. After each capriccio he took advantage of the applause to retune before launching into the next. He performed them in order, and virtually unconsciously. If he had favourites – and the fourth capriccio, which Schumann compared to the funeral march in Beethoven's *Eroica*, was it – one was unable to tell, for he played each as if it were his own, concluding with the majestic twenty-fourth that was itself a consummation of all that had gone before.

And although he accepted the audience's generous approval, which, to be honest, didn't really matter much anymore, and although he strode off like a Colossus, the restlessness and melancholy of the twenty-fourth capriccio nagged. He was also exhausted beyond anticipation. He instructed

Joel, his amanuensis, to keep the well-wishers at bay while he recovered in the Green Room, with one exception. A quarter of an hour had passed and he now began to sulk and fret. What he regarded as impossible seemed more and more likely with each passing gloomy moment. The din of the departing concert-goers had disappeared. At some point he would simply have to leave and thus acknowledge that everything had been for naught. Was he so ill a judge of human character, and of himself?

He might have snapped his Peccatte bow in half had Joel's friendly head not popped in, with its ridiculously arched eyebrows, as if to see whether the coast were clear, and the door swung open to admit Alessandra. She didn't look particularly happy, but then neither was the agitated Matteo, so he feigned surprise. She frowned, which only made her beauty more enchanting, and took a seat at some distance while he pretended to undo his bowtie.

'Thanks for coming,' Matteo said.

'You knew I'd be here,' replied Alessandra, 'at the concert anyway.'

'I was hoping for it.'

Alessandra was just a few years younger than Matteo, but she had aged far better, remaining athletic and graceful while Matteo had succumbed to the sedentary. The small muscles around her mouth quivered ever so slightly and she looked as if at any moment she would rise and slap him. Instead, she wondered aloud why he had mentioned Paganini's illnesses. Matteo shrugged and it was the shrug that broke the ice for her and made it easy to cross over and place a hand on his face, a hand he lightly kissed and which she immediately withdrew and which he just as quickly fetched and held.

It had been fifteen years since his last full performance of the *Capricci*, fifteen years since their rift, fifteen years of foolish meandering pain and anger, on both sides, and fifteen years for getting on with it, which for Alessandra meant husband, kids and orchestral career.

'I didn't think you were a sentimentalist,' said Alessandra, eventually withdrawing her hand.

'I'm not. Let's go for coffee.'

At the seedy fluorescently lit all-night diner not far from the hall and her hotel they ordered breakfast and drank several potfuls of coffee. And they talked. About her kids, her cello, about the husband who called her "Alex" but was a wonderful father; about Matteo's "chordal" as opposed to melodic affairs, which often resulted in trouble, and about Paganini.

'So what did you think – honestly?' Matteo inquired.

'A lot different from the last time, but I wasn't in the best frame of mind to hear them then.'

'And now?'

'They were genuine, Matteo, which is saying everything,' though she quickly added, 'but there were a few technical ... '

'C'mon, Alessandra, even HE couldn't play these damned things! And speaking of the damned, you're still damned beautiful. Whereas I know I'm not much to look at these days.'

'True. So now what will you do with yourself?'

'Teach, keep my hand in chamber, read, travel a bit. Enjoy what's left.'

'Enjoy what's left?'

'Just one night, Alessandra, that's all I need, that's all I want,' he whispered.

At her hotel, which she considered neutral ground, they disrobed and attacked each other with the ferocity of Paganini's bowing until they landed on the capacious bed, where they kissed long and desperately. Then of a sudden Matteo turned over onto his back.

'What's wrong?' inquired the cellist. 'How sick are you?'

'Very.'

'With what? Prostate? Lung? What's going on?'

'Nothing physical.'

'What do you mean?' she asked with suspicous anger.

'I'm sick of something I can't even define.'

Before the perplexed Alessandra could respond Matteo's words tumbled out in a torrent, gaining pace and urgency.

'We say we love things when we merely like or enjoy them, we say we're in love when we're consumed by lust, we say love is forever when everything changes all the time and half of those who swear it divorce. We put leashes on our lovers just to make sure they keep loving us back or else. Just what does loving someone mean? Smothering them, fawning over them, destroying oneself for them? We fall for people who ruin us, for people we know nothing about. Is that what love is, falling, falling, falling? It's killing me.'

'You're incorrigible, aren't you? And I fell for it.' Alessandra sighed, more in pity.

Matteo remained prone, gazing upwards at the ceiling, and extended his left arm to draw Alessandra close. She didn't resist.

'I need to talk, Alessandra.'

And so he did. He had no idea where the words came from, or how, or where they would lead, but he talked and kept talking and Alessandra listened and talked herself. They talked about their dimmest recollections, about popular songs, about their teachers, days at the beach when every worry could disappear, watermelon and mosquito bites and first cigarettes, boyfriends and girlfriends, about nearly being killed on the road, about funerals and the selfishness of the bereaved, and about how, when they had broken, each had found it hard to breathe properly for a year, and why they needed to hate each other to make it make sense. It was dawn before they had talked themselves out and Alessandra finally asked why he had refused her when she had been ready to give herself so wholly to him, when she had been ready to divorce, when she would have burnt her cello for his sake – or was that the problem, her giving?

'I was afraid,' Matteo answered dully.

'Afraid? We were so right for each other, you idiot! We liked the way we smelled, and tasted and felt, the way we could do nothing together, absolutely nothing, and enjoy it – which, by the way I have never been able to do with my husband, and you knew it! What were you so afraid of?'

Matteo hauled his naked body out of bed and returned with his instrument. He lifted up his bow and began to play the twenty-first capriccio, ever so softly, *amoroso*, all the way through. In the faint morning light, in his nakedness, he cut an absurd figure, like an ancient satyr without horns.

'To love you the way you deserved to be loved, I couldn't do this – or at least I thought I couldn't.'

'Come here, you silly man,' called Alessandra softly.

Their love-making – and isn't that a silly term, thought Matteo, to make what cannot be made but what just emerges – was tender, and in the aftermath of their *petit mort* they each had found immense release and comfort from the years of unsettled unresolved dis-ease.

'What now?' asked Matteo.

'Let's be capricious,' replied his lover mischievously.

And so with Matteo's finagling Alessandra gave a week-long series of classes to the Conservatory's cello students every second month. Her husband, who really had no choice in the matter anyway, accepted the curious arrangement, as did her canny teenagers when their mother's happiness was so evident.

Matteo Beauvoir, who in time visited nearly every music classroom in the city with his Guarnerius, stopped worrying about love, and began at last to enjoy it, whatever it was.

Caprice d'Adieu

The greatest evil always came about when I was most convinced of doing good. When, for example, I insisted on honesty from a lover, and being understood. Portia, before she cast me adrift, told me that what I really wanted was for her to stand under me, which she was no longer willing to do, and asked me why did her honesty always result in my anger, which I couldn't answer.

I stayed on in Parma after she and the rest of the quartet returned to New York. Our European tour had been successful: good reviews, good food, avid listeners and a minimum of after-concert inanities from the wealthy. We had two months before starting our next gig, a college residency for a music department in the Midwest. Two months in which Portia and I could come to terms with our personal separation and negotiate a professional relationship, two months to figure out independently whether we'd be able to continue working together as principal violin and violist. And no, I don't play viola.

As a musician she of all people should have understood – there I go again! – my *modus vivendi*, which was simply to create and live within, however rare and brief, those moments of beauty against which everything else in life pales. It was my only answer – to poverty, ennui, injustice, the messiness of loving, the State – my only motivation to keep at an impossible instrument in front of diminishing and aging audiences, my only refuge.

But now, I had no interest, in part because I had become very well aware of my limitations as a player, and try as I might to disavow the fact, I had reached a plateau. Even Portia made a crack about my tone after the Smetana, which hurt, though she was right. And at my age could I really improve? Yes, my left hand was excellent, but my bowing has always been deficient, though not for want of effort. As hard as I tried the fluid easy warmth of a singing line always eluded, even when at my best.

I wandered for days in and around Parma without much purpose in the aftermath of Portia's departure. Food, including the famous cheese and *funghi*, had no taste, and sleeping was difficult because of the summer heat. By chance I stumbled into the National Gallery, having wearied of the Parco Ducale nearby, where I had carted my untouched violin as if for company.

The museum was cool and I slowly and wearily made my way through, heavy of limb, unmoved by Correggio, Parmigianino, Bronzino, Holbein, Canaletto, Tintoretto, all that waste of colour, until as if by chance I espied the sketch of a young girl's head by Leonardo on my way out. I blinked, several times, and paused in wonderment before it: how could someone convey so much with so little? The glowing beauty of the woman's face – was she yet a woman? – with its suffering innocent eyes transfixed me and I had to be nudged out of the building by one of the museum guards at closing time. Back at my pensione I retched and could hardly catch my breath as the dreams came tumbling through and I knew no outlet save walking, a man without a family by choice, without a lover and now without the sanctuary of his art.

I must have been a sorry character in that lovely town, a gaunt dishevelled American toting a fiddle-case and going nowhere, but at least I'd had an idea, a solution even, that turned me around. We musicians all believe – we *know* – that technical deficiencies, above a certain level of expertise are really and simply deficiencies of *character*. There was never and could never be a division of mind and body; instead we were a whole. But the tricky part was how best to heal that whole. Correct my bowing, I reasoned, and the rest of the "me" would follow! How could I have ignored the obvious for so long? I know, I know – others might reason differently and suggest approaching the problem, for example, through some form of endless self-examination fostered by an expert paid a King's ransom over many years. Or homeopathy. But really, that was wrong side out.

With this epiphany came a measure of peace because I was further comforted by a historical example: Ciandelli. Allow me to explain. Gaetano Ciandelli was a cellist (of all things) rescued from mediocrity by none other than Paganini himself, a player moreover *whose bowing was deficient*. In three days – just three days! – the devil had worked a miracle and Ciandelli developed a tone that was beautifully pure, rich and graceful. Was it a coincidence that such a revelation should come to me in the city in which Paganini had once worked and was twice interred? Was it a coincidence that I had made my way to Leonardo's portrait in whose face was both the ideal for whom I strove and a mirror of my own sorrows?

I did what any sensible man would have done: I determined to elucidate Paganini's method by the most direct means. I roamed the outskirts of Parma until I had found my goal: a medium. Entering the candlelit interior of a fusty room I was greeted by a swarthy gypsy woman with Romani headdress and large dangling earrings. I excitedly confessed my woes and pleaded with her to use her powers to reach to that other side for the cellist (Paganini of course would be too much to ask for). Once I had satisfied her with everything I knew about Ciandelli, and with coin (figuratively speaking, because she actually took my credit card), she asked me to sit quietly while she begged permission of the spirits. Then she closed her eyes and moved her lips soundlessly for some minutes. Soon her breast began to heave, wildly, and she reached out for my hands, which I clasped in excitement and consternation. As she shook I trembled and a low melancholy wail issued from her lips. I was sweating profusely. Gradually she grew silent, released my grip and, sizing me up with her large dark eyes, uttered a single word: *ballare*. I attempted to ask for more specificity but she shooed me away imperiously, advising me not to return: 'Ballare! Ballare! Non devi tornare!'

I was exhausted when I fell into bed and, for the first time in a week, slept, and dreamed.

Reduced to poverty, and having only the clothes on my back, I wandered through Italy, France and Spain like a gypsy, playing my fiddle for sustenance. I reached Cadiz virtually penniless and I spent what little I had at a small café where I nursed a few bits of bread and wine. Then of a sudden a woman emerged out of the corner, taking small, slow and elegant steps. The few other patrons began to clap and before I knew it she was on a table swirling gracefully and percussively stamping a flamenco. When her face appeared to me in profile as she paused, I saw that it was the fanciulla of Leonardo now become a woman! How marvellous, yet how wrenching! She lifted her chin and I realised that she beckoned for my violin with her brightly gloved right hand. I demurred – the music was unknown to me – but I could not resist the command of her eyes, so I risked making myself a fool. She held her pose, her shawl uncovering shoulders and breasts of sublime shapeliness, until I had managed to begin. And then, and then! And then I played not knowing how except that I moved my bow in accordance with her dancing steps, lightly, rapidly, at greater length, sounding harsh at times or plaintive or sweet, but with a richness of tone that set the dancer's eyes aflame and the patrons alight. When she had finished, flushed from her sinuous exertions, I was called to her side for a bow, after which she wrapped her shawl around my neck and kissed me.

She brought me back to her modest home and allowed me to disrobe her – except for the elegant red glove that came near to her elbow – and to love. In the weeks that followed I played while she danced and I marvelled at my kinship for the music of that land, hearing in it the sorrow of the Sephardim and all the wandering gypsy tribes rent by hosts and invaders. But within my bliss I burned to know why she would never remove her glove, yearning for what it kept from my caress.

One day I told her I loved her so fully and so immensely that I would sacrifice anything for her sake.

She slapped me, hard, leaving the imprint of her gloved hand on my face, and sent me away. What had I done? When I returned some hours later, sheepishly, she informed me that we would not be performing that evening, that instead we would speak about my so-called love. Viola – that was her name – asked me why I thought I loved her.

'Because your beauty fills me with joy, because I would give you my all ... '

'And because you think I love you? Do you?'

I bowed my head.

'You are right, I do, but not the way you think. Let me tell you a little tale, a tale about a young girl, a young and beautiful girl who played the violin. Yes, did you not divine it? She met a man she loved so much she was beside herself, but he did not return her love in kind. Oh, he loved well enough, but not with his all, as you say. She was at pains to prove her love to him to set his full love free. But how? Why of course, with her violin! So one night, after surrendering her youthful self so utterly to her beloved's embrace, she fetched her violin and threw it into the fire, she a poor girl who could hardly afford a dress and who prized her instrument as a jewel, which in her hands it was. He laughed and scorned that sacrifice. 'A violin is a piece of wood you can acquire sometime again,' he said, 'what do you know of love?' As the flames crackled and the strings of my violin snapped I lifted my right hand for him to see, the hand that represented my talent, my very essence, which could not be reacquired, and fell upon my knees unclothed before the burning embers until I could bear the pain no longer and lost consciousness. And then what do you think happened, my dear American lover?'

My mouth was parched and I could barely utter a sound.

'He spurned me.'

I swallowed and gulped and shook.

'Do you still want to love me? Take this off and let's see what kind of lover you really are.'

She held out her arms and I took her hands with trepidation, the ungloved and the gloved, and kissed them, my tears streaming uncontrollably. I then slowly peeled the glove of her right hand downwards, instinctively turning my head away as I slipped it off and, grasping her elbow with my own right hand, girded myself for the unimaginable. When I opened my eyes I

saw, to my astonishment, a lovely unblemished and exquisite
hand and arm. I gazed at her bewitching eyes and fell upon her
naked fingers with my lips.

'There are many ways to dance,' she whispered.

My bedsheets were drenched when I awoke, and so real was
the dream that I searched in vain for Viola at my side. Immediately I retrieved my violin and attempted to repeat my
motions in the dream, dancing on the strings with my bow,
feeling every nuance of its weight with each finger independently, loosening my joints to a suppleness and ease instead
of flexion and rigidity. I thought of how the dancer's every
gesture was a miracle of efficient force: no unnecessary mus-
cle fired for her tableau.

I hurried to the *Fanciulla* of Leonardo. Not one superfluous line – all was ease and grace! After I had gazed my
fill I passed the remaining sunlit hours at the Parco Ducale
regaling passers-by with my capering bow and gypsy melo-
dies that poured from some unfathomed source. And then
another sound of strings, a distant busker growing near, now
answering in kind – another gypsy? Turning to welcome my
gleeful fellow-reveller whom should I see but Portia!

'I thought I might find you here,' she said. 'God, you look
awful!'

'But I feel great!' I replied.

'So now what?' she asked heavily. 'I can't go back to what
we were.'

'Neither can I.'

I decided not to tell her of voyages or dream, but raised
up the fiddle.

'Lend me your ear,' I implored, 'and nothing but, for just a minute. That's all I want from you. Nothing more, ever. And then let's get a bite to eat. I'm starved.'

Finis

About the Author

Emanuel E. Garcia is a poet, playwright, novelist and story-teller who currently resides in New Zealand. His most recent novel, *The Case of the Missing Stradivarius* was published in 2009 (Irregular Special Press: Cambridge, UK), and is now also available as an ebook. Two additional collections of stories will appear next year: *The Chronicles of Jasper and Gary (Accountants with Artistic and Amorous Ambitions)* and *Venetian Rogues*, both of which continue the saga of characters introduced in *Twenty Four Caprices for Violin*.